Rosett

Chistell Publishing

First Printing, March 2021

Published by: Chistell Publishing
                       7235 Aventine Way, Suite #201
                       Chattanooga, TN 37421

Cover: Blurberry Illustrations

ISBN: 978-0-9663539-5-2 (13-digit)

Library of Congress Catalog Card Number: 2020917313

chistell.com   1   by Denise Turney

Dedication

For my son.

I love you, Gregory –

Acknowledgements

Appreciation to the Source of all eternal creation.

Thank you to my family. My father, Richard Turney. My mother, Doris Jean. My son (and my heart), Gregory. My grandparents, Clyde and Emma. My great-grandmother Rebecca. My brothers, Richard, Clark and Eric. My sister – Adrianne. My nephew and nieces, Richard, Angel, Assyria, Samaria, Megan, and John. My aunts, Christine and Pat. My uncle Donald. My great-aunts Ruby and Marge. My cousins Donna, Monica, Michael and Langston. Thank you for a foundation of love.

To my friends and supporters. To those who read, support and enjoy my books. To my Sigma Gamma Rho sorors. To Tim and Essie Stackhouse, a woman who God used to allow the story of Ruth and Naomi to work itself into my life. To Helen Crawford (I'll never forget you walking around the corner those many times just to see how I was doing).

To everyone who has touched my life in a special way, including each person who has read my books, thank you for your love and support.

Be courageous and wonderful, loving YOU! -- Denise

Chapter One

"Mommy!" Rosetta screamed, the ends of her two thick braids blowing up. She ran through the living room waving her report card. "I did it!"

Lynda Blay, Rosetta's mother, turned away from her painting easel. The leopard painting that she was working on was coming along beautifully. "What is it?" she asked.

"I got three A's on my report card!" Rosetta screamed.

Lynda sprung from her chair. "Well, now," she smiled. "Looks like you're on the right track."

Her face plump with excitement, Rosetta ran around the living room corner. She raced inside her mother's art room, her report card flapping in the air as she held it up high.

"All the studying that I did paid off," Rosetta beamed. She hugged her mother around the waist. "Wait until Jennifer sees my report card." She kissed her mother's face. Then, she turned and ran out of her mother's art room. "She won't be able to leave me out of all the school clubs and keep telling everybody that I'm stupid."

"Rosetta," Lynda tried. "Don't you go showing off."

It was too late.

Not even two minutes passed before Rosetta plopped down on the living room sofa and picked up her cell phone. She called her best friend, Paulette. "That's right," Rosetta exclaimed into her cell phone. "I got three A's. I know I did almost as good as Jennifer."

"See," Paulette chimed, "I told you all the studying that you did would pay off."

"Yeah," Rosetta agreed. "You always know what to do."

"Pushing you to study hard every night instead of only once a week isn't tough," Paulette laughed. "I didn't do anything great. You're the one who did the hard studying."

"You just wait until Jennifer gets a look at my report card," Rosetta piped, circling the As on her report card with the tips of her fingers.

"Forget about Jennifer," Paulette coached. "The two of you have been fighting since elementary school. I don't care if you got straight A's for the rest of the school year, climbed to the top of Mount Everest and ran the mile in two minutes, Jennifer would still pick at you," Paulette laughed. "Jennifer just doesn't know how cool you are."

"Thanks, Paulette. You're my best friend for life."

"And, you're my best friend for life," Paulette said. "I love you like a sister. You and me, we're like blood relatives. Sisters."

"For sure," Rosetta cheered. "We've been cool since day uno. Remember when we went ice skating at the rink downtown?"

"We were so little then," Paulette said.

"Like five and six-years-old," Rosetta smiled, glancing up at the ceiling, as if recalling those early memories. "We had so much fun. Think we skated for a whole hour, falling down and getting back up," she laughed.

"On the way home, you talked your dad into pulling over and taking that injured mutt that we saw on the side of the road to the pound."

"I've always loved animals, Paulette. Couldn't leave that dog limping on the side of the interstate. Do you know that dog had a broken leg?"

"How do you know?"

"My dad told me," Rosetta answered, her hand going up and waving through the air. "I asked him to keep calling the pound. Guess what?"

"What?"

"That dog found a home in less than two weeks."

"Go, Rosetta! You've always rooted for the little guy. And, now you're getting your grades up."

"Thanks, Paulette." She pulled her cell phone closer to her ear. "Now, Jennifer," Rosetta continued, "She always thinks that she's a lot smarter than everyone, Miss Honor Roll. She's the teacher's pet."

"Who cares?" Paulette shrugged. "You're the fun one! You crack me up sometimes."

"Me, Gregory, Belinda and Anil like to have fun. Ms. Jackson doesn't care, though. She never notices me or anyone else in class," Rosetta groaned. She crossed her legs. "But wait until tomorrow," Rosetta piped, grinning at her report card. "I'm going to class first thing in the morning and shove my report card right in Jennifer's face."

The front door swung open. As it did, bits of snow blew off the porch onto the house's front entranceway. And cold air blasted into the living room. It felt like someone had turned on an ice fan. Cincinnati, Ohio's December temperatures were at record lows.

Rosetta's father, Robert Blay, smiled and waved to Rosetta while he walked through the living room into the art room where Rosetta's mother was painting.

"What's Rosetta talking about?" he asked Lynda after he greeted her with a kiss. Project demands at the marketing firm where he worked melted away. He was glad to be home.

Lynda chuckled at the question. Ten-year-old Rosetta was always up to something. It was hard for her mother to know what Rosetta was planning. Lynda figured that Rosetta made plans in her sleep. One thing was certain, Rosetta Blay, two long pigtails going like fresh vine down the sides of her head, was no one to ignore.

"I don't know," Lynda answered. "You know how that girl is."

"Well, she was on her cell phone saying something about a Jennifer when I walked through the front door." He paused. "Isn't that the name of the girl Rosetta got put in detention over? Remember?" he said to his wife. "Rosetta threatened to fight that girl two months ago." He shook his head. "Rosetta never got into trouble at school until that incident." He gave his wife a telling glance. "I say we find out what she's up to come dinner time."

"Oh," Lynda sighed, "Rosetta'll let us know soon enough. That girl can't keep a secret. She was probably on the phone talking with Paulette." She shook her head. "Goodness. When those two get together."

An hour later, the entire family was in the kitchen. Rosetta's older sister, Francine, sang Ariana Grande's hit song," Break Free" while she helped their mother cook a tuna casserole. As she sang, Francine rocked her head from side to side and filled the kitchen with sound.

At the edge of the kitchen counter, Rosetta tossed a chef salad. Her father set the table while

Rosetta's brother, Leroy, fed the family dog -- a Husky named Joe.

Francine, Leroy and Rosetta went to the same school, Harriet Tubman School on Fifth Avenue. Leroy was in the seventh grade. Francine was in the eighth grade, three grades ahead of Rosetta. As far as Rosetta saw it, she was in the grade that all the cool kids were in – the fifth grade .

"Rosetta," Francine stopped singing and frowned. "How many times are you going to toss that salad? Until the lettuce is as small as crumbs?"

"Mind your business?" Rosetta snapped.

"Cut that fuss out and sit down and eat," Robert told his daughters.

Rosetta took the salad to the table and sat down next to Leroy. He was two years older than she was, but he was her favorite person in the family. Leroy had the coolest fade hairstyle. And, he was a sharp dresser, rocking the coolest Dapper Dan jeans. He was so popular at school.

Rosetta loved her mother and father, but they were always finding her faults and letting her know about every one of them. "Sit up straight," they'd tell her. "Stop popping that gum," her mother would fuss. Chief of them all was, "Rosetta Blay, stop rolling your eyes."

Her parents told her that they were guiding her to become a responsible and joyous young woman. That's what they told her, but Rosetta wasn't buying it. To her, she was the kid in the family and everybody, except Leroy, picked on her.

Lynda sat at the kitchen table last. Before she sat, she laid a pan of seasoned broccoli on the table. Steam blew off the broccoli and warmed Rosetta's face.

Next, Lynda said grace. "All right, everybody, dig in," she chimed after she raised her head. "This tuna casserole looks delicious."

Rosetta pursed her lips. "Not if Francine put her hands on it."

Lynda looked at her youngest daughter. "Rosetta."

"All I know is that you better not go to school flashing your report card. I heard you on the phone with Paulette as soon as Leroy and I came home from school," Francine said. She grinned. "And this tuna casserole is scrumptious."

Rosetta ate her broccoli fast. It was one of her favorite foods. Then, she spent the rest of her time at the kitchen table playing in her tuna casserole. Her parents didn't fuss at her because she ate all of her broccoli and salad.

"Tyrone's cute," Francine said, changing the subject and talking about a new guy at Josiah Henson High School. "I know he likes me."

"Speaking of school," Lynda began. "Rosetta, what were Paulette and you talking about on the phone?"

Rosetta sat back in her kitchen chair. "Nothing important," she told her mother.

"Rosetta," her father admonished.

"Yes, Sir?" Rosetta asked, wiping her mouth with a napkin.

"Don't you go bothering that girl Jennifer or anyone at school. Understand?"

"Yes, Sir," Rosetta promised.

A second later, Rosetta rolled her eyes and worked hard to ignore her sister as she went on about the boy in high school.

"Tyrone asked if he could carry my book bag when we were walking to the bus stop this morning," Francine swooned, ignoring Rosetta's response to their father.

"I'm finished eating dinner," Rosetta announced. She couldn't stand another second of listening to her fourteen-year-old sister talk about the new guy. She hadn't seen him and she didn't need to. Besides, Francine was always liking some boy and talking about it like the whole world had to know. If Rosetta liked a boy, she wouldn't blab about it to the whole family. She'd keep it a big secret.

"Wash off your plate and you can go," Robert told Rosetta.

Lynda sipped her iced tea. "You barely ate the tuna casserole. Put it in the refrigerator. If you want a snack later, you can eat that casserole."

Rosetta put the casserole in a food storage container. Yet, she didn't plan on eating it -- not now, not tomorrow, not ever. On her way out of the kitchen, she grabbed one of the rice pudding treats that her mother had made last night.

She ran upstairs into her bedroom and grabbed her report card. "I'm not going to be real mean to Jennifer even though she's always mean to me. But," Rosetta grinned to herself. "Come tomorrow, if Jennifer picks at me, she's gonna know how good I did." She laughed. "She's gonna know that pretty soon I'm going to be the best one in class." She laughed. "I'll do anything to outdo Jennifer. I'll do anything to be better than her. Anything."

Chapter Two

Chatter filled the hallways of Harriet Tubman School. Center of it all was Rosetta. She told jokes about funny scenes from *Team Kaylie*, a popular television show that aired last night. Rosetta had students roaring with laughter until Ms. Jackson stood outside her classroom door and shouted, "Rosetta Blay! Get in this classroom right now!"

Jennifer ran behind Rosetta, taunting her with high pitched ridicule.

Seemingly oblivious to the teachers who stood outside the classrooms that lined the hallway, Jennifer ran with so much energy that she might as well have been outside. Mrs. Peterson, one of the fourth grade teachers, peered at Jennifer, but she didn't say anything.

Jennifer screamed in a sing-song way, "Rosetta's in trouble! Rosetta's in trouble!"

"Shut up, you—"

Ms. Jackson's brow went real tight. Her hands were jammed against her hips. She took her right foot and tap-tap-tapped it against the floor. "Rosetta Blay, get yourself in this classroom right now."

"But, Ms. Jackson, Jennifer was—"

"--Never mind about Jennifer," Ms. Jackson said while she turned and followed Rosetta inside the classroom. "You just concern yourself with Rosetta."

Seconds later and as if she hadn't hollered at Rosetta, Ms. Jackson walked to the front of the classroom with as much grace as a lake swan. She stood behind her desk and called roll. "Harold Abernathy, Billie Anderson, Amanda Barnes--" She scanned the room for raised hands while she continued to call the roll.

Just as Ms. Jackson was about to call out, "Rosetta Blay," Jennifer leaned across her seat, turned up her nose and whispered, "Is the dumbest girl in the world."

Rosetta hurried, raised her hand and called out, "Here." Then, she sat still. Jennifer and she had been at odds with one another since first grade. The way that Rosetta saw it, Jennifer disliked her because she was the only person in school who stood up to her, who didn't back down when she went on about how smart and blessed she and her family were.

"Dodo bird," Jennifer taunted in a low tone of voice.

Deep inside, Rosetta wanted to ball her hands into fists and shake them at Jennifer. Yet, she knew that if she did, Ms. Jackson would be at her desk in no time flat.

Next thing she'd know, Ms. Jackson would be marching her down the hall to the principal's office.

Jennifer wagged her head. She whispered, "Rosetta Blay has never made straight As on her report card because she's dumb." She rocked her head from side to side. When she did, the gold plated barrettes fastened to the top of her cornrows jiggled and gave off a shine. "Me. I always make straight As."

Rosetta froze. She sat as stiff as a pole. She was certain that her ears had deceived her. After all, her best friend, Paulette, had told her that *no way* did Jennifer get straight As this marking period. Paulette swore that she'd seen Jennifer's report card. She'd placed her hand across her heart yesterday afternoon and pledged, her back straight, her eyes fixed, that she'd looked right at Jennifer's report card.

"Jennifer's report card was hanging out of her Science book," Paulette told Rosetta while they sat next to each other on the school bus yesterday afternoon. "I saw all of her grades. She got two Bs."

Rosetta had never smiled so hard as she did yesterday when Paulette told her that. Paulette's revelation pleased her so much that she had started to laugh. That's when she devised her plan. Now, she wondered if she had gotten ahead of herself. Perhaps Paulette had been wrong. Maybe Paulette had wanted

Jennifer to stop getting straight As so much so, that she had imagined lower grades on Jennifer's report card.

Rosetta didn't have time to figure out if Paulette's eyes had played tricks on her yesterday. Jennifer was still leaning across her chair, the chair that Ms. Jackson had assigned her to three weeks ago.

"Dodo bird," Jennifer whispered again.

Rosetta sat up in her chair and stared at the blackboard. She tried hard to ignore Jennifer.

"You're so dumb, you're not going to pass to the sixth grade," Jennifer whispered into Rosetta's ear. "You'll be in school for the rest of your life."

Rosetta's hand shot into the air. She stretched her right arm so hard, her shoulder started to hurt. Students sitting close to her turned and stared at her. They watched her arm stretch and wave through the air.

Ms. Jackson faced the blackboard. She wrote words across the board in chalk.

Rosetta took her left hand, propped it against the elbow of her raised right arm and with a loud huff, she pushed her right arm into the air even further.

Ms. Jackson didn't notice Rosetta's propped up arm.   Ms. Jackson just stood at the front of the class writing on the blackboard.

Jennifer shot Ms. Jackson a quick glance. Seeing Ms. Jackson's back still facing the class as she continued to write on the blackboard, Jennifer leaned across her seat again. "Ol' dumb Rosetta can't make the Honor Roll."

Rosetta's eyes narrowed into slits. She clenched her teeth and told Jennifer to, "Shut up."

Next thing that Rosetta knew, Jennifer swung her leg out. She kept swinging her leg until the hard point of her shoe caught Rosetta's calf.

That's all that it took. Rosetta leaped out of her chair and eyeballed Jennifer. "Stop kicking me, Girl."

Ms. Jackson froze. Seconds later, she turned around. The first student who she looked at was Rosetta. "What's going on back there?"

Every gaze in the room fastened upon Rosetta.

Rosetta rolled her eyes and huffed.

"Rosetta Blay, pull it together or you're going to find yourself in the principal's office."

There it was -- the familiar threat of having to sit in the principal's office. It was an old threat; it worked, though. Rosetta returned to her seat and sat as still as a metal rod.

Ms. Jackson turned back around and faced the blackboard.

Jennifer started swinging her leg back and forth behind Rosetta's calf again.

"Stop it—", Rosetta began. Then, she felt Ms. Jackson's gaze on her. So, she closed her mouth, turned in her chair and looked at the blackboard.

"Okay, students," Ms. Jackson said. She held a stick of chalk in her hand. "Did everyone read the short bio on Harriet Tubman?"

"Yes," the students answered in unison.

"Good," Ms. Jackson said. "Jerome, please come to the board and write down the answers to the first five questions that I have put up."

Rosetta glanced at Jerome. He stood from his chair so slowly that Rosetta knew that he didn't know half of the answers to the questions. Before Rosetta knew it and although she tried not to, her shoulders were hunched over her desk and she was laughing.

"Um," Jerome began. He picked a stick of chalk out of the blackboard's bottom tray. He fiddled with his hands while he stood next to Ms. Jackson. Then, he looked up at Ms. Jackson and kept his voice low. The students heard him anyway.

Rosetta was no longer laughing. The classroom was so quiet that the students heard the heater humming in the background.

"Yes, Jerome?" Ms. Jackson asked. She smiled softly, a grin that came across as a trick to Rosetta. Because just as quickly as Ms. Jackson would smile at a student, if that student spoke out of turn or told jokes while she was teaching, Ms. Jackson would frown real hard and start shouting. Yet, her smile – it was sweet and it could pull you in.

Jerome pointed to the blackboard. "What's that word right there?"

"Maryland," Ms. Jackson told him. She stepped back and smiled. And she waited.

Several seconds went by. Jerome still held the chalk in his hand. There were no answers on the blackboard.

Ms. Jackson crossed her arms. Her smile started to fade.

Rosetta looked from Ms. Jackson to Jerome back to Ms. Jackson. Jerome was one of the cutest boys in class. But he never seemed to know the answers to many questions. He did much worse in school than Rosetta did.

Sometimes Rosetta felt sorry for Jerome. Sometimes she thought that Jerome got what he deserved.

A few weeks ago, Rosetta almost asked Jerome to go with her to see Francine act in a play at Josiah Henson High School, the school that Francine would be in next year. Josiah Henson had a bigger auditorium than Harriet Tubman School, enough to hold the twelve hundred people who had bought tickets to the after school play.

Never mind that Francine wasn't Rosetta's favorite person. Rosetta couldn't think of a better reason to make her way inside a high school and strut around alongside older kids like she was a big shot.

But she had quickly changed her mind. She'd been standing next to Paulette and Charlotte in line in the Harriet Tubman School cafeteria waiting to get a slice of mushroom pizza when, out of the corners of her eyes, she spotted Jerome grinning big. He was flirting with Ellen Montross, one of the prettiest girls in Harriet Tubman School. Ellen was also Jennifer's good friend.

That settled it. In no time flat, Rosetta told herself that Jerome was dumb, a waste of time and definitely not someone she wanted to be seen at a big time play with.

That was three weeks ago. Now, while she watched Jerome rock from foot to foot at the front of the classroom, Rosetta felt a smidgen of sympathy for him, but not enough to stop being mad at him.

"Maryland is a state in the United States," Jerome wrote slowly in a scraggly handwriting that was hard to read.

This time, Rosetta wasn't the only student giggling.

"Ssshhh, students," Ms. Jackson told the class.

After several long minutes, Jerome answered two questions. Then, he walked, head down, to his seat.

Ms. Jackson turned to the class. "Belinda, please come to the board and see if you can answer the questions."

Inches from his desk, Jerome looked at Ms. Jackson. His face was downcast, "Does that mean that I got the answers wrong?"

The students burst out laughing.

Everyone laughed except Belinda. She was heading to the blackboard and she didn't think that she knew the answers to the questions either.

Once at the blackboard, Belinda answered the first three questions. Then, she started rocking from foot to foot.

Ms. Jackson took the chalk away from Belinda and sent her back to her seat. She was frowning real good. "Did anybody study the text?" she wanted to know. Her voice turned loud. "Anybody?" She scanned the class. Her gaze landed on Rosetta.

"Rosetta," Ms. Jackson said. "Come to the board and answer the first five questions." She stopped. "No," she said. "Answer down to the tenth question. And I have to tell you all, just because you didn't know the answers to these questions, many which we covered in class last week, you will be reading more about Harriet Tubman. And you will be writing more on Harriet Tubman before we move along to cover another great abolitionist, Frederick Douglass."

Anil Kumar squirmed in his chair. He twisted his mouth. He looked like he had eaten a lemon. "I don't know why we have to learn about old people," Anil complained.

Some of the students nodded in agreement. "Un-hunhs" sprinkled the room.

"We weren't living back then," Anil continued. "That old stuff's not going to help us now. Nobody in our neighborhoods ask us about that old stuff."

The "un-hunhs" increased. Students nodded and looked at Anil. He seemed like the smartest kid in the classroom right now.

Ms. Jackson pulled up her lip. She looked sad. From where Rosetta sat, Ms. Jackson's back even looked slumped. For a second, Rosetta felt sorry for Ms. Jackson. She was so used to Ms. Jackson looking strong and in charge. She wanted her to go back to looking that way.

"History is important," Ms. Jackson began. "One day you will realize that. I'm sure if you asked your parents, they would tell you that history is very important." She searched the students' faces. "Think about your grandparents and great-grandparents," Ms. Jackson tried. "They are part of your family history." She smiled.

The students' eyes were wide. They stared at Ms. Jackson with amazement.

"Why don't we have a history event for the upcoming talent show?" Rosetta suggested from her chair. She still hadn't walked to the blackboard. She grinned big. She was pleased with her history event suggestion.

Ms. Jackson's brows rose. She smiled approvingly. It was a look that Rosetta hadn't seen from Ms. Jackson in weeks, since she had brought a stray kitten off the playground into class. She had walked the cat to the principal's office with Ms. Jackson. From there, they had called the local animal shelter and turned the cat in. They kept up with the cat. A week later, when they called the local animal shelter, they found out that the cat had found a loving home.

Ms. Jackson's smile encouraged Rosetta to continue. "We could ask our parents and grandparents questions. We could draw pictures, write poems, dance, sing songs and make short speeches based on their answers."

The look of surprise on Ms. Jackson's face turned into outright shock. "Rosetta," Ms. Jackson beamed. "That is a wonderful idea." She turned and faced the class. "What do you all think?"

Everyone except Jennifer nodded their agreement. Jennifer put her head on her desk and sighed. She could kick herself for not thinking of the idea first.

Ms. Jackson glanced at Jennifer, her star pupil.

Jennifer continued to sit with her head on her desk.

"I saw all those nods," Ms. Jackson said. She alternated between glancing at Jennifer, glancing at Rosetta and looking at the entire class. "Your family history projects will need to be turned in no later than Monday. We need time to prepare for the talent show that's on Tuesday two weeks from now." She glanced at Jennifer, a tall, slender girl with a gentle smile. "To be certain that the class wants to have a family history event for our school talent show, let me see a show of hands from everyone who is in favor of the idea."

Every hand in the class went up, every hand except Jennifer's.

Rosetta didn't care. She knew that hers was a great idea. She loved the idea for two reasons. It made her the star of the class and it took Ms. Jackson's focus off of the questions on the blackboard, the last place that Rosetta wanted to be.

Chapter Three

"Help me roll the snow into a bigger ball," Malcolm Baxter, a ten-year-old neighbor shouted to his brother, Terrence, and six neighbor friends. Their gloves were wet with slushy snow. The huge snowball that they pushed was four feet tall and three feet wide. The boys and girls laughed and ran, thumping and bumping each other, while they pushed the snowball bigger.

It was three-thirty in the late afternoon. Snow fell out of the sky like cold cotton. Although it was winter, the sun shined in the sky. Front lawns filled with eager kids who busied themselves making snowmen or playfully sliding on foot across the slick sidewalks.

If Rosetta wanted to, she could race outside and join her friends. Instead, Rosetta stayed indoors. She had other plans.

She had been home from school for ten minutes. Never one to sit still for long, Rosetta jumped off the stool that she'd been sitting on in her mother's art room. She walked to her mother's side.

Joe wagged his tail and walked next to her.

Lynda painted a long, light stroke of sky blue across the top of the sketch paper. Below the blue were rows of palm trees and brown sand. "Rosetta, you look like you want to ask me something," Lynda turned away from her painting and asked. "What is it?"

"Can we go over Grandma and Pop Pop's?"

Lynda brushed more strokes of sky blue paint across the top of the paper. "Which ones?"

"Grandma and Pop Pop Fleming."

Lynda smiled. "What about Daddy's mother and father?"

"I only have so much time to get ready for the school project. And guess what?" Rosetta added. She didn't give her mother time to respond. "The project was my idea and Ms. Jackson and the whole class loved it." Her mouth drew down. "Everybody except that dumb Jennifer."

"Now, Rosetta—"

"--No, Mommy. Jennifer doesn't like anything I do. While everyone was excited about my idea, Jennifer sat with her head on her desk."

"Honey, maybe she believes that her value is determined by others. That could cause her to seek to be the center of attention."

"Yes," Rosetta mumbled while she turned her foot on its side. A second later, she asked, "What does that mean?"

After she placed her paint brush in the water cup next to her chair, Lynda turned and gave Rosetta her undivided attention. She smiled softly at Rosetta, her youngest child.

"It means that maybe Jennifer isn't sure that she is valuable. So, she needs other people to constantly show her that she is. Thing is," Lynda continued, "Unless Jennifer comes to see her own value for herself, all the cheering and approval from everyone else will never be enough."

Lynda recalled the times when she had been uncertain of her value. She looked at Rosetta. She didn't say anything. However, she wondered if Rosetta struggled with that same challenge from time to time.

"I guess," Rosetta sighed. Then, she took in a deep breath and beamed, "So, can we go?"

"We'll see. First, what is the project? Why do you have to go visit your grandparents tonight?"

"It's for the talent show at school. The show is in two weeks. I have to learn about my family history," Rosetta told her mother. "Ms. Jackson said she wants us to have our project done by Monday."

Lynda asked, "Are you sure that Ms. Jackson didn't give the class more time to prepare?"

"No," Rosetta said with a shake of her head. "We just have this weekend. Ms. Jackson doesn't fool around. We have to get moving."

"Well," Lynda said. "That doesn't give us much time."

"I'm only going to ask Grandma and Pop Pop three to four questions," she told her mother.

"Gotta keep them from rambling," Lynda smiled. She stood, "Right now, I say we go in the kitchen and see what Daddy has for us. It's his turn to prepare dinner." She followed Rosetta out of the art room. "I'm sure he has something delicious."

"Well, hello, ladies," Robert said as Rosetta and Lynda entered the kitchen. He placed a large bag from Baked Food on the kitchen table. He still had his coat on.

Joe ran up to Robert, barked and wagged his tail.

"Smell that grub, don't you?" Robert piped to the family dog, Joe.

"Are you just getting in from work?" Rosetta asked. She neared the table and peeked inside the large bag. "Salmon." Her eyes lit up. "My favorite."

Robert smiled. "I thought about that while I was at the restaurant. And, yes," he nodded at his youngest daughter, "I'm just getting in from work. Office closed early today due to the snow."

Lynda neared her husband's side and kissed his mouth. "Rosetta and I are heading out to my parents and then to your parents after dinner."

"Why are you going over there?" Robert asked. He pulled a large dish of corn out of the restaurant bag.

"Rosetta has a school project—"

Rosetta put the salmon platter on the table. "--It was my idea," she beamed. "Ms. Jackson asked us to come to the board and answer questions about Harriet Tubman."

The front door opened then closed. Francine came through the door first. Leroy was on her heels. The scent of food hanging in the air led them straight into the kitchen.

"Good," Francine said. "We got home from basketball practice in time."

"You know that we'd wait longer for you two before we started eating," Lynda said, looking from her oldest daughter to her son.

"I was scared Rosetta was going to eat up all the food," Francine snickered.

Rosetta rolled her eyes. It was hard being the youngest in the family. But Rosetta was tough -- she could handle Francine. Yet, this time instead of arguing, Rosetta turned away from Francine.

"As I was saying, Mommy and Dad," Rosetta continued. "The questions were about Harriet Tubman."

Lynda chimed, "Harriet Tubman is my heroine."

Rosetta's face filled with surprise. "You should have been in class today." She twisted her mouth. "I would have aced that in-class assignment. That ol' Jennifer would have been embarrassed to see me outdo her."

"Rosetta."

Rosetta glanced at her father. "I know. I know," she said. "Focus on yourself." She looked up at her father. "I knew you were about to say that." She twisted her mouth.

"And one day you will heed that good advice." He smiled back at her. "Then, you won't hear me say it again."

"Ro-Ro-Set-Your-Head--" Francine sang.

"--Don't call me that," Rosetta blurted, cutting her sister off.

Francine cackled until her shoulders shook. "Baby Ro-Ro, you're so jealous, it's sickening," Francine frowned. "You're always worried about what someone is doing." She clucked her tongue. "Jealous. Jealous. Jealous."

After she gave Francine a *that's enough* look, Lynda took plates out of the cupboard. "Let's sit down and eat so that we can get started on Rosetta's project."

"What are you working on at school?" Leroy asked. He was genuinely interested in the project. He was proud of how Rosetta was maturing. He remembered when she was a cuddly toddler following him around the house, carrying her favorite toy, a cotton doll that their Grandma Blay had made for her.

While Rosetta placed drinking glasses on the table then grabbed silverware out of the drawer below the sink, she kept talking. "Nobody in class knew all of the answers to the questions Ms. Jackson put on the blackboard about Harriet Tubman. " The table set, she eased into a chair and served herself salmon, corn, spinach and sweet potatoes. "I knew some of the answers though."

After Lynda said grace, Rosetta took a bite out of her salmon. "I didn't think that I was going to know the answers to as many of those questions that Ms. Jackson put up on that board as I did."

Oh, the safety of home for Rosetta. She thought that she could lie about events that happened at school without anyone discovering the truth.

"Rosetta, you're smart," Robert said.

Francine grunted.

Rosetta ignored her sister and kept talking. "I know, Dad. I just forgot that Ms. Jackson was going to ask us questions about Harriet Tubman. We read a book about Harriet Tubman last week," she said.

"So what is this project for school all about?" Robert asked.

Chapter Four

"Ooo-wee!" Pop Pop Fleming screamed as soon as he saw Rosetta and Lynda. He leaned forward in his chair and welcomed his daughter and granddaughter into his home. "What brings you two by on this cold December day?"

Rosetta rushed inside her grandfather's arms. For the last two years, she had told herself that she was too old to be running inside her grandparents' arms. Yet, each time that she saw them, her heart got so happy that she couldn't help herself.

"We wanted to see Grandma and you," Rosetta answered. "And," she continued, "I have a school project."

Pop Pop glanced at Lynda. "What's this all about?"

Then, he glanced at Rosetta. She was nearly up to his shoulders. Rosetta was tall. Pop Pop also knew that Rosetta was equally as mischievous. As far back as he could remember, Rosetta always seemed to be up to something.

"Ms. Jackson loved my idea," Rosetta beamed. She hurried further inside the living room. "Where's Grandma?"

"She's upstairs looking through her closet," Pop Pop laughed. "She's trying to pick something out to wear to a banquet that we're going to tomorrow night."

"What's this banquet for?" Lynda asked after she kissed her father on the cheek. She walked to the living room sofa and sat. "You two are always going somewhere."

After he stood and reset the security alarm next to the front door, Pop Pop sat on the sofa next to Lynda. "I told you how our colleagues from the College of Downtown Cincinnati keep in touch with us. Some of them still work at the college. Well, the school is having an alumni banquet."

"It's wonderful that you and Mom met where you work."

Lynda leaned to the side on the sofa, toward the living room stairs. "Rosetta," she called.

Pop Pop waved his hand. "Leave her be," he said. "She's upstairs spending time with your mother. You know Elaine's in her glory to have Ro with her." He leaned back on the sofa. "How are Francine and Leroy?"

Lynda sighed. "They're fine, but those kids get on each other's nerves." Lynda pursed her lips. "Well, all except for Rosetta and Leroy. Those two have always gotten along. But Rosetta and Francine get on each other's nerves at least a dozen times a day."

"No," Pop Pop said. He shook his head. "We aren't going to have that. And," he added, "Francine should know better than to pick at Rosetta. I've seen those two. Francine starts most of the arguments." He looked at Lynda. "What is it about Rosetta that you think Francine wants?"

Lynda snapped her finger. "Now, that's an idea. I hadn't thought of that before. Rosetta has a lot of fire." She twisted her mouth. "Francine has a lot of fire in her belly too. So, I don't think that's it." She snapped her finger again. "Maybe Francine is jealous of the fact that Rosetta's the youngest in the family."

Pop Pop laughed. "No. I don't think that's it. Francine likes being in charge too much to want to be the youngest. I think she might be a tad jealous of Rosetta's spunk and courage. Both girls have plenty of fire in their bellies. That's a good thing. Francine reacts to what people say to her. That's when I see her fire. Rosetta, on the other hand, starts a lot of things with her fire. That's the difference that I see in them." He nodded. "You know, Francine might wish that she used her fire to start things instead of responding to what others start."

Lynda shrugged. "You might be right."

When they stopped talking, they heard Grandma Fleming and Rosetta's voices coming down the stairs.

"How long did Pop Pop and you date before you got married?" Rosetta asked on her way down the stairs. She walked in front of her grandmother. She pushed loose strands of hair behind her ears and ran her tongue around her mouth. She sounded like a newspaper reporter.

"Two years," Grandma Fleming said. "Marrying your grandfather was one of the best things that I've done."

Rosetta smiled. "You two do make a good couple."

Pop Pop and Lynda laughed.

"She's full of questions this evening," Grandma Fleming said. She walked to the sofa and sat next to her husband. "Thanks to Rosetta, I picked out the gown that I'm going to wear to the banquet tomorrow night."

"It's a pretty green dress," Rosetta said. "Grandma has a lot of long, pretty dresses in her closets. I've never seen so many dresses before, all shiny and glittery," Rosetta added. "Grandma said that when I'm a grown woman, I can pick some dresses out of her closet and keep them as my own."

"Now that's a deal," Pop Pop said. He looked at his wife. "And what are all these questions that Rosetta's been asking?"

Grandma Fleming looked at Rosetta before she turned and met her husband's glance. "She was asking me about when we met, how we met and what I love to do. Questions like that."

Pop Pop Fleming looked at Rosetta. "Why are you so curious?"

"I told you," Rosetta said. "My teacher -- Ms. Jackson -- she loved my idea. We were answering questions about Harriet Tubman. Nobody knew the answers to all the questions. So, Ms. Jackson told us how important it is that we know our history, even for things that happened a long time ago. So, I suggested that we focus on family history during our talent show. We have to ask our parents and grandparents about their lives when they were younger. We have to ask them what family means to them. Stuff like that," she said. "So, I want to ask you questions that I came up with for the project." She pointed at her chest. "It was my idea and Ms. Jackson loved it."

"This Ms. Jackson means a lot to you, doesn't she?" Pop Pop asked while he watched Rosetta sit in a chair on the other side of the living room.

Rosetta rocked her head from side to side. "She's my teacher."

Grandma Fleming tapped her husband on the forearm. "You know how it is at that age," she told her husband. "Everything a teacher says sounds like the gospel."

All the adults in the room laughed.

Rosetta watched their faces scrunch up while they laughed. For as long as she could remember, it made her feel happy when adults in her family laughed. They always seemed so busy working, shoveling snow, washing dishes, folding laundry, mowing the lawn, cooking and painting. It was like they never sat down and laughed. Having fun just didn't seem to be on their long list of things to do.

Ms. Jackson was the same way, now that Rosetta thought about it. She wondered if it was an "adult" thing. If it was, Rosetta was glad to be a kid. The only trouble that she had at home as a kid was with Francine. But she could deal with her. She knew that their parents didn't want them to fight. Yet, if Francine kept picking at her and coming up with smart aleck remarks, Rosetta just might haul off and punch her good. She could only take so much of her sister's criticisms.

Then, there was her arch nemesis, Jennifer Davis. Between Jennifer and Francine, Rosetta didn't need one other troublemaker in her life – ever.

"Okay," Rosetta announced. "Time for the questions." She pointed at her grandparents. Then, she stood and grabbed a spiral notebook off her grandparents' dining room table. She already had a pen. It was stuffed inside her pants pocket. She'd carried it from her parents' house over to her grandparents'.

"So," Rosetta said as soon as she returned to the living room. She sat in the chair again and crossed her legs. "Grandma, when you met Pop Pop did you want a family?"

Grandma Fleming sat back on the sofa. "Goodness. I was only seventeen years old when I met your grandfather. I had just gotten a job at the College of Downtown Cincinnati as an analyst in the admissions office." She laughed. "I wasn't thinking about starting a family then. I was just starting to come into my own." She raised a finger. "As a matter of fact, I was still living with my parents."

"But I worked my irresistible charm on her. . . ."

Never minding that her grandfather was busy talking, Rosetta interrupted him with, "--Pop Pop, did you want to have a family when you met Grandma?"

"Not right away," he answered. "All I wanted when I first met your grandmother," he said while he turned and looked at his wife, "was to be with her. . . ."

Rosetta wrote fast.

"--Thanks, Pop Pop," Rosetta smiled. She pulled the spiral notebook further up on her lap. "Just a few more questions," she said. "What is the number one thing that makes a family strong?"

"That's easy," Grandma Fleming said. "Love and genuine concern for every person in the family."

"Yes," Pop Pop nodded. "That and the willingness to let each person develop into her or his authentic self."

"Well put," Lynda exclaimed to her father. "I love how Mom and you put things." She looked at Rosetta. "How many more questions, Ro? Because we have to get moving to Grandpa and Nanny Blay's if you're going to get all of the answers that you need to your questions tonight."

"Just two more questions," Rosetta said, clearing her throat. "What is the one aspect, and it can only be one, that you appreciate most about our family?" She turned and looked at Pop Pop. "Ms. Jackson thought of that question," she grinned.

"I appreciate you the most," Pop Pop leaned forward and rattled off. His eyes were big and sparkly when he answered her.

Rosetta knew that he was teasing. She also knew that deep down he meant every word that he spoke. She knew that she was one of her grandparents' favorite people.

"Pop Pop," Rosetta pleaded in a sing-song way.

"You and the courage that the folks in our family have," he answered.

"Grandma?"

"You and our family's sense of humor."

"Okay," Rosetta said. She kicked her legs out. Then, she quickly pulled them in toward the bottom of the chair again. "Last question." She glanced up at her mother. Then, she looked at her grandparents. "What do you want most for our family now and forever?"

"I want everyone in our family to achieve their deepest dreams, because like Langston Hughes said," Pop Pop shrugged. "Who knows what comes of a dream deferred?"

"What's that mean?" Rosetta wanted to know.

"It means who knows what happens to a person who has to keep waiting for her dream to come true."

"Langston Hughes implied that the long waiting for a dream to come true may hurt a person deeply over time," Grandma Fleming added.

Lynda stood and draped her purse over her shoulder. "Okay, Rosetta. Let's get off to Nanny and Grandpa Blays'."

Rosetta jumped to her feet. "Not yet," she begged. "Grandma hasn't told me the one thing that she wants for our family now and forever." She smiled softly and looked across the living room at her grandmother who smiled softly back at her. "Grandma?"

Grandma Fleming sat back on the sofa like she had all night to answer Rosetta's question. That is, until her daughter, Lynda, looked down the bridge of her nose at her, at which time Grandma Fleming pushed forward on the sofa and waved her hand. "Oh, don't go rushing me," she told Lynda. "This question deserves a real good answer."

Chapter Five

"Come on in," Nanny Blay said, rolling her eyes. Her voice was flat. She seemed bored.

Rosetta and Lynda followed Nanny Blay inside her well cared for house. As usual, the leather furniture and the expensive china and Denox knick-knacks looked just like every strand of Nanny Blay's hair always looked – exactly where it should be. There was no dust on the furniture. All of the satin sofa pillows were fluffed and placed in their usual spots on the sofa.

Without much conversation, Rosetta and Lynda followed Nanny Blay inside her kitchen.

Nanny Blay leaned her hands on the kitchen table. Then she paused, as if she was inspecting the yellow sugar jar at the table's center. Next, she walked to the refrigerator, opened the door and pulled out a gallon of white milk and a bowl of rice. "So, what brings you two over tonight?"

"I'm doing a school project," Rosetta told her. She knew how inquisitive her grandmother was. So, before she got the chance to start rattling off a string of questions, Rosetta added, "I have to ask you and Grandpa questions for the project and I don't have long."

Lynda gave Rosetta a sharp glance.

"Oh, so they are teaching you children something over at that school," Nanny Blay laughed. She glanced across the room at Lynda. "I always told your father to put you kids in a private school." She looked away from Lynda, put the bowl of rice in the microwave and rolled her eyes. While the microwave table spun and heated the rice, Nanny Blay shook her head. "Can't get anyone to listen to me anymore." She looked at Rosetta. "Your father used to listen to me."

"Nanny," Rosetta tried. "Is Grandpa here?"

"He ran to the bakery to get one of those lemon cakes that he likes so much." She sighed. "You and your mother won't get mad if I sit down and eat myself some of this here rice, will you?"

Rosetta sat in a kitchen chair with her knees on the cushion. She leaned her elbows on the table top. "Go ahead, Nanny. We're good. Unless," she added, looking at her mother who stood just outside the kitchen doorway, "Mommy's hungry."

"No," Lynda said with a shake of her head. "I'm fine. We ate before we came over." She glanced inside the living room. She still had her hands jammed to the bottoms of her coat pockets. "I'm going to go in the living room and sit on the sofa." She looked at Nanny Blay. "Is it okay if I go in the living room and watch some television?"

"What are you going to watch?"

Lynda couldn't resist. "*Sesame Street*," she teased. When Rosetta met her glance, she winked.

"Well," Nanny Blay said with a wave of her hand. She looked down at her rice which she had recently taken out of the microwave and cooled with some of the milk. "I suppose it can't hurt." She waved her hand again. "Go ahead. Help yourself."

With that, Lynda was gone.

"Okay," Nanny Blay said while she sat down at the kitchen table. "Finish what you were telling me about this school project. I want to know what the project has to do with me."

"Well," Rosetta began. She still sat in the chair with her knees propped against the cushion.

"And get your knees out of that chair," Nanny Blay said. She swiped Rosetta gently across the shoulders. "You know better than to sit like that."

Rosetta sat down real proper. "No one in class knew the answers to all the questions that Ms. Jackson asked." She quickly added, "I knew most of the answers to the questions that she asked me though." She knew how big Nanny Blay was on making straight As in school.

"After all those questions, my teacher, Ms. Jackson, told us to create a history project."

"Let's get started," Nanny Blay said. She talked fast, like she was in a hurry.

Half an hour later, Rosetta carried her spiral notebook close to her chest, snug against her wool coat. She walked in step with her mother out of her paternal grandparents' house back to the car.

"I'll tell Robert that you both said hello," Lynda waved before she closed the car door, shutting out the night's cold.

"Bye, Nanny," Rosetta waved. Her mother and she weren't halfway down the side driveway when Nanny Blay turned abruptly and closed the front door. When she did, a long icicle fell off the roof into the front yard with a loud plunk!

Chapter Six

"Bbrrii-nngg!" The alarm clock blared at the side of Rosetta's bed.

Rosetta rolled to her side and slammed her hand atop the radio, shutting off the noisy alarm. Then, she rushed inside the bathroom.

Monday couldn't have come soon enough for Rosetta. She couldn't wait to show Ms. Jackson her parents' and grandparents' responses to the history questions. The experience found Rosetta pondering becoming a journalist. The local newspaper sure could use her smarts, she thought to herself as she washed her face and brushed and flossed her teeth.

Back in her bedroom, she pulled on a pair of black knit pants and her purple blouse, the one with "You're a star" stitched across its front. Rosetta had done more than just ask her parents and grandparents questions. She'd pulled the raw goods out of them. She was pleased-pleased-pleased with herself.

Then, just-like-that, Francine peered inside Rosetta's bedroom. "Why are you getting dressed so fast?" she asked Rosetta. Francine wore her cute green and black stripped skirt set, the one with the fluffy white blouse that Rosetta liked so much.

"I gotta get to school and start working on the talent show," Rosetta grinned.

Francine laughed. "Just make sure that you don't start making stuff up to make yourself look like a big shot."

Rosetta rolled her eyes. "Mind your business," she said just before she grabbed her coat and headed out of her bedroom.

Francine laughed louder. "You say that now." She followed Rosetta down the stairs. The heels of Francine's shiny, black knee high, leather boots made a pop-pop-pop noise each time they landed against a step. "You're not in school struggling to put a decent talent show together yet."

Leroy and their parents were already in the kitchen. Rosetta smelled the scrambled eggs, grits and turkey sausage as soon as she entered the kitchen. She thought that her mother was the best cook in the world. Her mother's food always tasted good. And, it smelled like a chef had cooked it.

Breakfast, as usual, was full of conversation and lightheartedness. Rosetta's parents sipped green tea while they ate. Rosetta, Leroy and Francine drank freshly squeezed orange juice with their breakfast. Everyone erupted in laughter each time Robert, his sense of humor in full swing, told a joke. It was the one time in the day when the family was sure to be together. As hard as Lynda tried to have her family together at the dinner table, after school academic and sports events kept them from making it home right after school on more than a few occasions.

"Have a good day, Sweetheart" Robert called out to Lynda half an hour later, after he grabbed the garbage and headed out the front door for work. His children followed him outside.

Lynda stood at the doorway kissing and hugging her children and husband. She went to her toes when Rosetta, the last person to exit the house, stepped off the porch. Joe stood next to Lynda, his thick coat warming him, his tail wagging.

"I love you all," Lynda said, waving to her family as they walked away from the house. "Rosetta, let me know how Ms. Jackson likes the answers you got for your school project when you get home."

Moments later, Francine, Leroy and Rosetta were on the school bus. As usual, they sat next to their good friends, kids they'd chummed around with since they were knee high.

Rosetta sat next to her best friend, Paulette Jones. Paulette was a year older than Rosetta, so she was in a different class, but that didn't matter. As soon as the girls sat, they started talking about Disney's *Andi Mack* television series. It was one of their favorite television shows.

"Hey, Paulette, did you catch Andi Mack last night?"

"For sure I did," Paulette answered, smiling and turning toward Rosetta. When she crossed her legs, her left foot kicked her leather pink, plaid push-lock purse that lay on the bus floor next to her.

"Do you believe that Bex is Andi's real mother?" Rosetta asked, pulling her book bag up further on her lap.

"Yeah," Paulette answered. "Even though Bex looks young, she's old enough to be Andi's mom. Remember?" Paulette said, tapping Rosetta's forearm. "Bex was a teenager when she had Andi."

"I don't want to have kids until I'm in my thirties," Rosetta smiled. "There's so much that I want to do before I even think about getting married and starting a family."

"Like what?" Paulette chuckled, leaning into Rosetta's right shoulder.

Rosetta leaned toward Paulette and smiled. "Like going to college. I want to be a veterinarian. I love animals."

"Cool."

"And, I want to travel," Rosetta added, looking at Paulette.

"Like where?"

"Africa, Italy, Australia and Tokyo, for starters," Rosetta said. After a pause, she asked, "What about you, Paulette? Do you want to start a family young like Andi's mom did?"

"No way," Paulette said. "I'm like you. I want to travel a lot, except I want to go to Africa, Spain and India."

"You should be Buffy in *Andi Mack*," Rosetta laughed. She tightened the grip on her book bag when the bus rolled over a series of bumps in the road, causing the school bus to shake and bounce.

"Buffy's mom was in the military. Talk about a cool way to work and be able to travel all over the world," Paulette said.

"And Buffy is a super cool friend for Andi," Rosetta said.

"She is," Paulette agreed, glancing out the bus window at passing cars. A second later, she turned toward Rosetta and said, "Cyrus is a super cool friend too."

"He is," Rosetta nodded at Paulette. "And, I like his courage," Rosetta nodded. "You gotta have good friends."

"For sure," Paulette said.

The rest of the bus ride, all Rosetta and Paulette did was talk about last night's *Andi Mack* episode.

Then, the bus stopped in front of the school, and the girls hurried off the bus. After Rosetta waved good-bye to Paulette in the school hallway, she hurried inside Ms. Jackson's classroom.

Jennifer was standing at the door wearing a pair of black and red plaid pants and a white wool blouse. "So, did you finish your dumb project?" she asked Rosetta.

"Did you do anything besides study this weekend?" Rosetta crossed her arms and asked. "You probably don't have two real friends. So, all you can do is study."

Seconds later, Ms. Jackson walked into the classroom. "Okay, students, we have a lot to cover, so take a seat. After I call roll, we'll review the reading assignment that I gave out for you to complete over the weekend."

"Reading assignment," Rosetta thought to herself. She didn't remember a reading assignment. All

she knew about was the great idea that she had for the talent show. If she didn't know any better, she would have thought that Ms. Jackson was lying.

To Rosetta, roll call was going faster than normal. She fumbled through her book bag for her notepad, anything that would remind her of the reading assignment. This made two straight weeks that she had forgotten to study an assignment. If she kept it up, her grade was going to fall. She knew that if she brought home one more C, she was going to get grounded. She wouldn't be able to play with Paulette after school or on weekends. She wouldn't be able to talk with her friends on the telephone. That was too much. Before Rosetta knew it, she was scheming, something that she was far too good at.

"Anil," Rosetta whispered. She leaned back in her chair. "If Ms. Jackson calls me to the board, tell her that you want to answer the question—"

"--Un-unh," Anil said with a shake of his head. "I'm not going up there. I didn't do any reading over the weekend."

"Belinda," Rosetta tried, glancing to her right.

Belinda sat up straight. Her head and gaze were focused on the blackboard. She acted like she didn't hear Rosetta calling her.

"Belinda," Rosetta begged. She reached inside her book bag for a piece of cherry flavored taffy candy, Belinda's favorite. "I've got four of these," Rosetta beamed. She whispered, "I'll eat two and you can have two if you go to the board if Ms. Jackson calls on me."

Belinda didn't so much as glance at Rosetta.

"Everyone's here," Ms. Jackson said after she called roll. She smiled and scanned the room. Her gaze landed on the only student who was busy talking – Rosetta.

"Rosetta," Ms. Jackson began, "Since you had a great idea for our class talent show, why don't you come to the blackboard? You can review the reading assignment that I gave out last week."

"But," Rosetta whined. She glanced from Anil to Belinda. "I was just called to the board on Friday." She looked at Anil and Belinda one last time, then she glanced toward the ceiling and begged a silent, "Help!"

Ms. Jackson waited.

It was like Rosetta's feet were stuck in cement. No way was she getting up. One glance to her left and she saw Jennifer grinning from ear to ear. When Rosetta saw Ms. Jackson peek at Jennifer, she kicked herself. She didn't know how she could have gotten sucker punched and believed that Ms. Jackson was pulling for her last

Friday when she told her that it was a good idea for the students to ask their family history questions for the talent show.

Over the hum of the heater, Rosetta heard Jennifer snicker.

Rosetta clenched her teeth and frowned. Before she knew it, she stood. The only problem was that her knees were knocking together. Halfway to the blackboard, her heart started racing and her hands were shaking. She wondered if her knees were going to bang together until she fell to the floor.

"Did you like the story?" Ms. Jackson asked Rosetta.

Rosetta nodded in quick jerky motions, the kind of head nods that let her parents know that she was lying, but the kind of head nods that Ms. Jackson hadn't seen often enough to know what they meant.

Ms. Jackson leaned forward. She examined Rosetta's face. "Rosetta?"

"Ye-Ye-Yes," Rosetta stammered.

"Mr. Barber was quite the character, wasn't he?" Ms. Jackson smiled. She grinned so big that if Rosetta hadn't known better, she would have sworn that Ms. Jackson had just won a prize.

Rosetta turned around until her back faced the class. She turned so far that Ms. Jackson couldn't see her face anymore. Rosetta didn't answer. Instead, she stared at the blackboard.

Ms. Jackson looked at Rosetta's back with raised eyebrows. Something about Rosetta didn't seem right to her. The usual spunk that Rosetta moved with was missing. "Okay, Rosetta," Ms. Jackson said. "We're not going to write answers to the questions on the blackboard. So, you can turn around and face the class."

A few students snickered.

Rosetta's knees knocked together that much faster, that much harder. She spun around. Her feet crisscrossed. She nearly toppled to the floor.

Snickering rose, became louder.

Rosetta's gaze swept the room. She stiffened her spine, pushed out her chest and twisted her mouth. She could hear Nanny Blay telling her to, "Stand up and give an account of yourself."

"Yes," Rosetta nodded like a drill sergeant when she looked at Ms. Jackson. She was Rosetta Blay and Rosetta Blay wasn't scared of anybody.

Ms. Jackson looked at Rosetta standing tall and stiff and she pinched back laughter. "Rosetta," she said,

"What is the main character's name in <u>Sun, Shine on My Face</u>?"

Rosetta's gaze darted. It was as if, by moving her eyes, she thought that the answer would come to her. After several awkward seconds, all Rosetta could think to answer was, "All of them."

The class burst out laughing.

Rosetta pinned her hands behind her back. She still stood tall and stiff. She looked for Charlotte and Gregory, two of her classroom friends.

Charlotte sat with her blouse pulled up over her mouth, a sign that she was trying hard not to laugh. Gregory hung his head over his copy of <u>Sun, Shine On My Face</u>. Everyone else was guffawing, their mouths open wide, their heads tossed back, their shoulders quaking.

Charlotte and Gregory had just passed a very important test. Because they weren't roaring with laughter like the rest of the kids, Rosetta counted them as sure friends.

"Ssshhh," Ms. Jackson told the class. "Rosetta," she said. "There was one main character in the story. Tell us the main character's name."

"Why, don't I know the character's name?" Rosetta wanted to ask out loud. But, then, in her

imagination, she saw Grandma Fleming's finger wagging in her face and she held her tongue. She took a lot of time answering because she was sure that she didn't know the right answer. "Maaa-rriillee Trruu-gannnn."

"Did you say Marilee Trugan?" Ms. Jackson asked just to be sure that she had heard Rosetta correctly.

Rosetta clenched her hands. She was terrified to have the wrong answer. If she did, she knew that the class would roar with laughter, twice as loudly as they had before. "Yes," she said.

"That's right," Ms. Jackson smiled. "That's right," she repeated.

Jennifer sunk down in her chair and rolled her eyes.

Ms. Jackson asked Rosetta another question. "Where did the Trugan's live and would you say that their lives were easy or hard?"

Rosetta's confidence started to go up. "They lived on a farm down South." She turned her foot on its side. "I don't remember the name of the town," she admitted. "But the woman who wrote the book's name is Evelyn Pierce." She grinned real big. "She's a good writer."

Jennifer stuck out her tongue. When Ms. Jackson turned away from Rosetta and faced the class, Jennifer quickly pulled her tongue back inside her mouth. But Rosetta saw her.

"There was a lot of racial tension that went on in that story," Rosetta blurted. She didn't wait for Ms. Jackson to ask her another question. She wanted to prove to everyone, and especially to Ms. Jackson, that she knew what she was talking about.

"The injustice is real bad in the story," she shook her head, "Horrific in some areas. Marilee goes out of town and sees how bad it is. People just don't treat her right. A Black man gets hurt. It's just not good. Marilee Trugan and her family feel all of this." Rosetta's face went down. She looked sad, like she was Marilee Trugan and was remembering all the bad things that had happened to her and her family.

Ms. Jackson looked at Rosetta wide eyed. "Very good, Rosetta."

Yet, Ms. Jackson wasn't finished. When Ms. Jackson opened her mouth again, Rosetta almost dropped to the floor. She couldn't believe that Ms. Jackson was going to ask her another question. The longer that she stood at the front of the class, the more Rosetta knew that Ms. Jackson was on Jennifer's side.

Why Ms. Jackson would like a mean girl was beyond Rosetta. She knew one thing for certain now. Ms.

Jackson liked Jennifer more than she liked her. She told herself that's why Ms. Jackson kept asking her questions. She wanted to stump her. It made Rosetta so mad that she frowned until her forehead hurt. But there was nothing more that she could do.

Ms. Jackson smiled at Rosetta. This time her smile looked tight, curt, to Rosetta. She closed her eyes to keep Ms. Jackson from seeing her roll them.

"What do the Trugans do for a living?" Ms. Jackson asked.

Rosetta was still rolling her eyes when she opened them.

Silence went over the room.

Rosetta looked up at the ceiling. Then, she looked down at her feet. She looked at the classroom door. Then, she looked out the window. She didn't dare look at any of the students. She could feel their gazes locked on her. The room felt hot, like somebody had turned the heat way up.

Ms. Jackson waited.

Rosetta looked at the door again. She wanted to run, bolt out of the door. But there was nowhere to go. Even if she got all the way down the hall, Ms. Jackson would call Mrs. Laurice Brown, the school secretary, and have her brought back inside the school and marched right to the principal's office, a place Rosetta never wanted to go to again unless it was to receive a special commendation or award.

Ms. Jackson tilted her head to the side. "Rosetta?"

"Ah-Ah," Rosetta stammered. "They were horse trainers," she said. A second later, she shook her head. "No," she said. "They were grocery store owners."

Ms. Jackson nodded. "Right," she said. "And who owned the property that their grocery store was on?"

"Ms. Jackson," Rosetta finally asked. "Why are you asking me so many questions?"

A surprise greeted Rosetta. The only person in the class who laughed after she asked the question was Jennifer. It was like all of the other students wondered the same thing.

Ms. Jackson stepped back. "I'm asking you questions because I want to make sure that you read the story and also because," she smiled, "I know that you know the answers." She paused. "I'm not picking on you." Her face softened. "I want you to do your very best." When she spoke again, her voice was firm. "Now answer the question. Who owned the property that the Trugans grocery store was on?"

"A man named Ho-How," Rosetta began. Her hands were clasped behind her back. "Howa—"

It wasn't long before Rosetta picked up that Ms. Jackson's wide opened eyes signaled that she was on the right track.

"How-ard," Rosetta finally said.

"Right," Ms. Jackson beamed. She raised a finger. "One last question."

Rosetta let out a deep breath. She exhaled so hard, the ends of her braids blew up.

"Just one more question," Ms. Jackson assured her. "Why are the Trugans indebted to Mr. Howard?"

"They owed him money." It was a total guess, but it worked.

"Right, Rosetta," Ms. Jackson said. "They had borrowed money from Mr. Howard. Very good," she nodded and told Rosetta. "You studied good for today's class. I'm proud of you."

Rosetta walked back to her desk with her head high. She didn't miss a step until she reached her seat.

That's when Jennifer leaned across her chair, frowned and snipped, "You cheated, and I wish I knew how. If I did, I'd report you to the principal. You'd be in

Principal Greene's office in no time flat." She wasn't finished. "And that great idea you had last Friday. It's going to go all wrong," she assured Rosetta. She laughed and sat up straight. "Watch what happens," she forewarned. "Your talent show project is going to be horrible! It's going to bomb! I'm going to make sure of it!"

Chapter Seven

"Woof! Woof!" a neighbor German Shepherd barked.

It was early Tuesday morning, the day of the school talent show. It was so early that the sky was dark reddish orange. Rosetta lay on her bed and peered out her bedroom window. Every now and then, she heard a neighbor call out "good-bye" to her spouse. Then, she heard the neighbor click her way down the front walk to her car and another day of work.

Across the hall, Rosetta heard her father stir. He normally got out of bed first in their family.

After she heard her father scoot into the bathroom, Rosetta climbed out of bed, an hour earlier than she normally did. She parted the curtains and looked outside. From where she stood on the third floor of her family's home, Mr. Jones, their next door neighbor who was busy scraping ice off his car windows, looked small.

Ice stuck to the windows of all the cars parked on the street. Smoke billowed out of house chimneys. The neighborhood stray dog, a small brown and black mutt, raced from beneath a car.

Rosetta watched it all happen. She laughed at the dog while she watched it run. She couldn't count the times that she'd begged her parents to let her keep the dog. As far as Rosetta was concerned, the dog was a friend.

A second later, Rosetta turned away from the window and walked around the side of her bed to her dresser. She pulled out clean underwear and a new training bra. Then, she went to her closet where she stood for ten long minutes trying to decide what to wear to school.

She could almost kick herself for not asking her parents to take her to the Tri-County Mall over the weekend so that she could pick out a new outfit. A week ago, she saw a pair of straight leg jeans and a pretty purple and yellow sweater that she knew she'd look cute in.

Finally, she settled on a pair of black nylon pants and a long orange, sparkly sweater that reached to the tops of her thighs. Her father no longer in the bathroom, Rosetta grabbed the undergarments and hurried into the bathroom. She wanted to practice what she was going to say at the talent show before she went into the kitchen to eat breakfast.

She washed up fast. She was out of the bathroom in no time flat. As soon as she grabbed her pants and sweater, she heard her mother stir in her parents' bedroom across the hall.

"Robert," she listened to her mother say. "Will you put a pot of tea on the stove while I take a shower?"

"You got it," she heard her father tell her mother.

That's what Rosetta liked about her parents. They shared.

After Rosetta dressed, she smiled approvingly at herself in her bedroom mirror. This was her day. She was going to be the standout student in front of the entire school. All of the teachers at Harriet Tubman School were going to marvel at her.

"My family is from Virginia," Rosetta whispered to her reflection in the mirror. She didn't want her mother to overhear her and ask what she was doing up so early. She definitely didn't want to wake that meddling Francine. It was enough that she had to spend the weekend listening to Francine sing the songs that she'd perform in school later today as part of the eighth grade project. So what, Francine had a gorgeous voice. To Rosetta, Francine sang too loudly and too much. Besides, Leroy practiced his class project over the weekend too, but he was cool about it. He didn't practice at the top of his lungs the way that Francine did.

Rosetta continued to whisper as she stood in front of her bedroom mirror. "Virginia," she repeated. "That's the first place that my family came to when we were kidnapped and forced to America from Africa." She stopped. She looked hard into the mirror at herself. Except for her smooth, brown skin, she couldn't see where she was African. But that's what her parents told her. Even her grandparents told her that, and they were old enough to know for sure.

"We're from West Africa," her grandmother Blay told her last night when she called her to get more details about her family for the class project. "Ghana," her grandmother Blay went on. "We are a proud people," she told Rosetta, her voice growing deeper, firm. "You tell your school that."

Rosetta heard the smile in her grandmother Blay's voice. She loved her grandmother. She just thought that her grandmother Blay was too tough, too strict. She wasn't easy going like Grandma Fleming.

Returning her attention to the mirror, Rosetta practiced and said, "My ancestors understood time by observing the sky. They knew how to take root right out of the earth and create healing medicines. They didn't have a lab or a doctor telling them what to do. They knew," she pointed to her heart, "in here, exactly what to do." She exhaled. "My family is still that way. That's how my grandparents and parents faced challenges when they were younger. They listened," she placed her hand against her heart, "to what they heard inside themselves and they followed that even if people told them that what they were doing was wrong." She smiled. "And it turned out good."

Footsteps echoed outside of Rosetta's bedroom door. "Rosetta," Lynda asked, "Are you up?"

Rosetta cracked the door and peered out at her mother. "I'm practicing for my school project."

"Oh," her mother smiled. "Then, go on. Don't let me bother you." She paused. "Do you want me or your father to drive you to school this morning?"

Rosetta thought for a moment. "No," she said. "I'll catch the bus like normal. I don't want anyone to think that I need special stuff for today."

Lynda grinned and left Rosetta to herself.

Rosetta practiced her speech two more times, then she headed for the kitchen. Halfway down the living room steps, she smiled. Not a sound. That meant that Francine was still asleep. "*Maybe,*" Rosetta wondered "*I can eat breakfast and get on the early school bus before Francine wakes up.*" That would be a sure sign that the school project was going to be a huge success.

Determined to catch the early bus, Rosetta hurried downstairs to the kitchen and scrambled herself two eggs and ate a slice of toast for breakfast. She washed the food down with a tall glass of orange juice.

Breakfast eaten, she reached for the dishwashing liquid and dish rag. It took her less than two minutes to lather and rinse her saucer, drinking glass and fork and place them in the dish drainer on the right side of the sink.

Just before she grabbed her book bag and headed for the front door, she pulled on her winter coat and walked out back, a heavy bag of bird food tucked in the crease of her right arm. With her left hand, she held Joe's leash.

Joe wagged his tail and looked for a spot in the backyard to pee. While he did, Rosetta walked to the barren cherry tree in the center of the back yard and, opening the bag of bird food, she poured the food in the double sided feeder that was placed atop a pole beneath the tree. In the summer, when the cherries were a ripe red and purple, Rosetta, Francine and Leroy picked the cherries to eat. Most of the cherries they placed in buckets and gave to their mother to freeze or to make a cherry cobbler with. That was also the time when the birds ate more cherries than bird seed.

Winter cold changed that. Now, it was as if the birds looked to Rosetta to help feed them, a responsibility that Rosetta, a true animal lover, was honored to accept.

Freezing temperatures stung Rosetta's face and hands. Soon she turned and said, "Come on, Joe." Pulling on Joe's leash, she resealed the bag of bird food and headed for the back porch.

Lynda was in the kitchen when Rosetta walked up the back porch steps and re-entered the house. "Thanks for feeding the birds and taking Joe out this morning," Lynda said, patting Rosetta's back.

"You're welcome," Rosetta smiled, washing her hands at the kitchen sink.

Half an hour later, Francine ran down the living room stairs just as Rosetta and Leroy followed their father out of the front door. The fact that she had dodged her sister's pestering this morning put a smile on Rosetta's face. She laughed her way out of the house.

"Have a good day," Lynda called out to Rosetta and Leroy as they walked to the bus stop at the end of the block.

Leroy walked alongside his neighbor and friend, another sixth grader named Maxwell. Rosetta walked with her good friend, Paulette.

"Be great at the talent show," Lynda added. "I can't wait to hear how it went when you get home."

Outside on the snowy sidewalk, Paulette bumped Rosetta's shoulder. "You're going to be fantastic," she chimed. "I can't wait to hear you speak at school later today."

Rosetta grinned so big, the corners of her lips turned way up, making her mouth look like a perfect half moon.

Behind them, Robert tapped his car horn, sending a beep-beep echoing across the snow-covered yard. He waved to Lynda, then he shifted his car from reverse to first gear and inched his way down the street. When he neared Rosetta, Paulette, Leroy and Maxwell, he rolled his window down. "Knock it out of the box at the school talent show today."

They waved and smiled back at him. Then, he pressed his foot on the accelerator and sped down the street. In the distance, Rosetta and Paulette saw their yellow school bus approaching.

Leroy and Maxwell ran onto the bus ahead of the girls. As usual, they sat all the way at the back of the bus where the older kids were.

"Hi, Mr. Miller," Rosetta said to the bus driver while she stepped to the side and let Paulette board the bus ahead of her. The bus' steps and main landing were covered with slush.

"Good morning, ladies," Mr. Miller responded to Rosetta and Paulette.

"Oh, boy," Byron Long, a red-headed freckle faced boy who loved to pick on Rosetta said as soon as he heard her voice. He craned his neck and tried to see around Paulette. "It's Rosetta," he announced. He tossed his head back and let out a rip roaring laugh. "It's the girl with the dumb braids who's going to ruin the talent show for the fifth grade ."

Rosetta nearly pushed Paulette to the bus floor, she raced so hard to the middle of the bus where Byron was sitting. "Shut your mouth—"

Mr. Miller stood from the driver's seat. "Rosetta," he said in a raised voice. "Go find a seat and leave Byron alone."

"Didn't you hear what he said to me?" Rosetta demanded. Now she had two people to be mad at this morning and one of them she liked. She didn't want to argue with Mr. Miller. But she wasn't going to be blamed for trouble that she didn't start.

Mr. Miller waved his hand. "Please just go find a seat," he told her. "Everyone needs to be seated before I can pull away from the curb and get you all to school on time."

Rosetta searched both sides of the aisle for a seat.

When Rosetta looked at her, Paulette raised her hands and shrugged. "I just barely found this seat myself," she said. Then, she pointed to a seat two rows behind where she sat.

Rosetta followed Paulette's pointing finger. The only open seat was next to Ellen Montross, a girl Rosetta didn't think that she'd ever like even if they both lived to be one hundred years old.

Paulette peered over her shoulder toward the back of the bus. She chuckled when she saw Rosetta standing with a blank face next to Ellen. That is until Rosetta met her glance.

Rosetta's face drew down. She looked sad. Then, her brows tightened and she looked mad.

Mr. Miller glanced into the rearview mirror. "Rosetta."

Rosetta crossed her arms and placed them hard against her chest. She turned away from Mr. Miller and stared out the window.

"Rosetta," Mr. Miller said. His voice took on an edge. "Sit down. We cannot leave until you sit down."

"Come on, Ro," Leroy called out.

Rosetta went to sit down next to Ellen.

Mr. Miller closed the door, put the bus in first gear and pulled away from the curb.

As soon as she was certain that Mr. Miller was focused on the road, Ellen thrust out her hip, forcing Rosetta off the seat.

"Thump!" Rosetta's body sounded against the bus floor.

All of the students and Mr. Miller turned. What they saw was Rosetta sitting on the aisle floor, legs pulled up and her books spilled across her lap.

Mr. Miller pressed the brakes so hard that the students lunged forward. Rosetta slid across the floor from the back to the middle of the bus. Her eyes were big when she stopped sliding. The first person that she looked at was Mr. Miller. His face was tight.

"Get up," Mr. Miller demanded. He stared so hard at Rosetta that her forehead felt hot.

Rosetta went to point, but Mr. Miller shouted and she got sidetracked.

"It's nobody else's fault that you decided to sit on the floor," Mr. Miller told her. "You wanted to do what you wanted to do. You are so stubborn," he added with a tight frown.

The words hurt. Rosetta thought about fighting back, but one look at the frown on Mr. Miller's face and she knew that arguing would only get her in more trouble.

When she turned around and looked at Leroy, she saw that he was so busy joking with Maxwell and his other friends that she doubted that he even heard Mr. Miller fussing at her. Seeing no other recourse, she pushed off the bus floor and wiped the back of her pants. She couldn't go to school looking a mess, especially not today.

She stood and slid across the bus seat, next to Ellen.

Ellen folded her arms tightly across her chest. Then she huffed and stared directly ahead. She didn't look at or speak to Rosetta once. *"If you thought that hip push was bad, wait until you get to school,"* Ellen mused while she cut her eyes at Rosetta.

The bus headed toward Harriet Tubman School faster than it normally did. Bumps in the road made for a rocky ride.

Mr. Miller breathed a sigh of relief each time that the bus made its way through a green light that was starting to turn yellow. The sooner that he got the bus and the students to the school, the better. This was one of those mornings when he wondered why he kept his job. Sometimes students, particularly strong willed kids like Rosetta, worked his patience.

And he liked Rosetta. He thought that she was a sweet girl. But she had a will like iron. No one could tell her what to do. Sometimes Mr. Miller wondered what Rosetta's parents let her get away with when she was at home.

"Alright," Mr. Miller said as soon as he pulled in line behind a row of other buses. "We're here." He glanced into the rearview mirror at the students. "Be respectful of others as you walk off the bus. No pushing," he added. "No shoving."

The students marched off the bus, one behind the other. Finally, Rosetta reached the front of the bus.

"Rosetta," Mr. Miller said when she passed him. "I didn't mean any harm when I told you to get up off the floor. I wasn't picking on you."

Rosetta looked at him – hard. Then, without saying a word, she turned and walked off the bus. She didn't care how badly Mr. Miller felt after he accused her of doing something that she did not do. She wasn't going to smooth the wrinkles out of his conscience with a nod and a grin.

"Paulette," Rosetta called after she stepped off the bus and rounded the corner.

Paulette was standing at the front of the school. She wasn't going anywhere until Rosetta caught up to her. They were friends for life. "You're still going to have a good day," Paulette told Rosetta while she pulled her wool hat further down over her head.

Rosetta thought that Paulette's black wool hat, purple and burgundy-colored feathers dangling around the hat's front edge, was pretty. To her, Paulette dressed stylishly, like a first-rate model who was still in grade school.

"You're dope," Paulette smiled. "You're gonna be the GOAT at the talent show," she assured Rosetta.

"Thanks, but why do you say that?" Rosetta asked. "I don't need a pep talk." A second later, she peered over her shoulder at the bus which was slowly making its way behind a row of buses on the other side of the school. "Oh," she sighed. "Mr. Miller." She didn't give Paulette time to say another word. "Ellen pushed me to the floor." She thrust her hip out the way that Ellen had done on the bus. "She poked out her hip, hard too," she added. "And she pushed me on the floor. Mr. Miller blamed me because he knew I didn't want to sit next to Ellen. But," she was quick to add, "I didn't just plop down and sit on the floor."

The girls' faces looked like plump half moons while they laughed their way to the school's main entrance.

As soon as Paulette swung the glass school door open, Rosetta and she heard a myriad of voices. The hallway was filled with chattering, laughing students and a few teachers who ordered, "Get to class."

Rosetta walked to the end of the hall to Mr. Anderson's classroom, the class Paulette was in. Paulette and she stood outside the classroom chatting. Before they knew it, the school bell rang.

"I bet your Grandma Blay told you a lot of good stuff," Paulette said.

Rosetta twisted her mouth. "She did, but you know that she doesn't like my mother."

They grinned, at each other. They bumped shoulders and spoke in unison. "In-laws."

"Hey," Paulette tapped Rosetta's shoulder and said, "I heard if the school talent show's good, Mrs. Greene is going to have us present the talent show to the entire city."

Rosetta clapped her hands. "That's so Gucci."

They both laughed.

"That means that Leroy'll get to see me perform twice," Paulette said. She grinned real big.

Rosetta waved her hand. "Leroy's too old for you. I keep telling you that."

Paulette pursed her lips. "He's only one year older than me," she sighed. "That's not a lot. And besides, I like him. I don't care if he is your brother." She clucked her tongue and rocked her hips. "And that's that." She added.

Rosetta turned. She walked back down the hall to Ms. Jackson's classroom, the ends of her braids bouncing as she went. She laughed all the way. If she only knew what lay ahead of her.

Chapter Eight

The auditorium was packed, lights beaming. The stage's newly cleaned floor length, red velvet drapes looked elegant, like they belonged on TV at the *Kids' Choice Awards*.

The eighth grade class, the highest grade at Harriet Tubman School, presented first. Even though she didn't want to admit it, Rosetta knew that Francine was going to get a standing ovation. Yesterday, Francine told Rosetta that she was portraying Betty Jones, a famous 1940's jazz singer. If anyone could portray feisty Betty Jones, it was Francine.

Besides having great acting skills, Francine could flat out sing. She sang popular Kierra Sheard, Rihanna, Ariana Grande and Selena Gomez songs around the house.

"Students," Mr. Marks, an eighth grade teacher, called out. He stepped away from the red velvet drapes and moved to the center of the stage where he stood behind the microphone. He spread his arms wide. His voice bellowed across the auditorium. "Thank you for coming," he smiled. "And now," he announced, "we present to you the Jazz Pioneers."

Students and teachers clapped. Many of the students leaned forward in their seats, especially those who sat at the back of the auditorium. They wanted to get a closer look at the stage.

"The Jazz Pioneers," Mr. Marks shouted.

The heavy red velvet drapes opened. A cardboard 1940's backdrop of downtown New Orleans came into view. Francine and nine other students stood on stage. They wore wigs and stylish black shoes.

Rosetta's mouth swung open when she saw Francine dressed in their Grandma Fleming's black and white cotton dress and black and white feathery hat. A string of pearls went around Francine's neck. A smaller string of pearls wrapped around her right wrist. To Rosetta, Francine looked elegant.

Francine took in a deep breath, then she belted out, "I've been living and striving for a mighty long time. The cowardly way ain't never been mine. I tell you I'm a foot stomping, no prisoners taking kinda woman."

More students scooted to their seat's front edge. Francine's voice and her brazen attitude had them hooked.

Rosetta leaned back in her seat and grinned. Forget the arguments that Francine and she had at home, her big sister was singing her heart out on stage and, Rosetta was suddenly pleased as punch about that.

Francine rocked her hips from side to side. She pulled the pearl necklace up with a flip of her hand and sang, "So I'm gonna have myself some fun and do what I want for as long as I feel like it."

A curtain further back on the stage opened and the rest of the eighth grade class chorused, "Yeah."

Francine strutted across the stage. She walked with so much confidence that she appeared cocky. She sang for ninety whole seconds. Then, she extended her right leg, leaned back on her left hip, pushed the floor microphone under her bottom lip and bellowed, "New Orleans, I love you. You're perfect for me. You let me dance. You let me soar. You let me sing. You let me be me. That's why I'm gonna shine for you."

Francine extended her hands to the audience. Large stage lights beamed on her. Right now, she thought that she was a star and she felt like one too.

"For you, I give my all. For you," she shook her head until the ends of her wig brushed back and forth across her shoulders, "I sing. I dance. I soar." She held the next note for what seemed like a minute. "For you."

Next, Francine spun in a circle. The black and white dress that she wore flew up. She tapped her way across the stage, the heels of her shiny black shoes landing against the floor fast and in a jazzy rhythm.

When she stopped tapping, she bowed her head, but only for a second. As she raised her head again, she peered into the students' and teachers' faces and started on the eighth grade class' second song. She sang "You Stir My Joy," as if it was her signature song, as if she was twenty years older than she actually was.

The eighth grade Jazz Pioneers performed for thirty minutes. They received a loud and long standing ovation as they left the stage. Chants of "Francine! Francine!" rang out.

Then, the seventh grade class went onto the stage. Myra Singh, a tall outspoken seventh grader, pushed her wheelchair up the ramp at the side of the stage. She stayed next to Leroy and her other good friend, David Chin.

Tom-tom drums sounded at the back of the auditorium. Every student and teacher turned and looked toward the auditorium's back doors.

Bobby James, a boy who was sweet on Francine, pounded the drums. He kept glancing out of the corners of his eyes for Francine while he pounded the drums.

As soon as Rosetta saw Bobby, she turned back toward the stage. She was surprised when she saw Francine peering around the stage curtain.

Francine looked at Bobby.

Rosetta grinned. *"I knew it. I knew it,"* she thought to herself. *"Francine likes Bobby. She doesn't like Tyrone."*

But that's not what Francine vowed while they were at home and Rosetta pushed her on the issue. "Bobby is a sweet little boy," Francine would say, her long Afro locks dipping to her shoulders.

"I like Tyrone Baxter, the sophomore at Josiah Henson High School," Francine told Rosetta the few times when they were home alone and didn't argue. "Tyrone and I are soul mates." It was some new phrase Francine came across in a woman's magazine. "We're meant to be together," Francine told Rosetta.

At the end of the seventh graders' performance, the sixth graders took the stage. Twenty-eight minutes later, as the sixth graders took a bow, another noisy round of applause went up in the school auditorium.

Rosetta stood, craned her neck and tried to see the stage. But there were too many students standing in front of her.

"Rosetta. Rosetta," Gregory tapped Rosetta's arm and said. "It's time for us to go on stage."

Chapter Nine

"Excuse me," Rosetta begged her classmates, their backs turned toward her, while she made her way toward the stage. She felt like sticking her arms out and pushing everyone out of her way. But she knew that wasn't a good way to start what she was sure would be the best class presentation.

Charlotte, Lynette, Belinda, Anil and Michael, kids Rosetta had gotten along with since kindergarten, stepped to the side and created an opening for her to walk through.

Jennifer was six people in front of Rosetta. She stopped walking as soon as she saw the hole that her classmates had created for Rosetta. She frowned, stepped to the side and filled up the space.

Rosetta turned and waved to her five classmates as she passed them, walking thru the opening that they had created for her. "Thanks, you all," she said. Her head was still turned when she rushed forward. She slammed right into Jennifer's back.

All of the students fell forward, nearly landed on the floor.

Ms. Jackson turned from the edge of the stage and faced the class when she heard the commotion.

"Stop pushing me, Rosetta," Jennifer yelled.

"I have to get on stage," Rosetta argued.

Mrs. Greene, the school principal, sat on the front row with a stern look on her face. She pulled down on her suit coat and folded her arms across her chest. No other class had found trouble and now here the fifth graders were struggling just to get onstage.

"Rosetta!" Ms. Jackson screamed. She jammed her hands against her hips and frowned at Rosetta.

Everyone in the auditorium turned and looked at Rosetta.

Rosetta froze. She didn't know what to say. She didn't know what to think. The class project was her idea. She couldn't let the project fall apart. She couldn't.

One look at Ms. Jackson and every fifth grader froze. The fifth grade students knew that once Ms. Jackson got mad, it was hard to turn her nice again.

Jennifer twisted her mouth. She thought fast.

Another look at Ms. Jackson and Rosetta nearly ran onto the stage.

The fifth graders wore long expressions. They felt sorry for Rosetta. They knew how much the school project meant to her. They also knew that Rosetta was always getting into trouble.

Jennifer glanced at her classmates. There wasn't one fifth grader who she didn't look at. Their faces told her a lot. Every one of her classmates was on Rosetta's side. After all that had happened, they were on Rosetta's side.

Jennifer frowned. If there was one person who she couldn't let outshine her, it was that bothersome Rosetta Blay. She stiffened her spine and went into high gear.

"Come on, Rosetta," Ms. Jackson said through clenched teeth. Ms. Jackson stood center stage gripping the silver microphone pole.

After Rosetta stumbled onto the stage, she looked out into the audience. A gaze at the corner of the stage caught her attention. It was Francine.

Francine looked at Rosetta and did the most unusual thing; she smiled. All at once Rosetta's mind started to race. She didn't know what to think. Francine . . . being nice to her.

Rosetta turned away from Francine and looked into the audience. She spotted her brother, Leroy. He wore the red and black long sleeve Jordan sweater that Rosetta bought him for his birthday two months ago.

Leroy gave Rosetta a nod. He smiled a slow sure smile at her.

It was all that Rosetta needed. While she stood on stage, in her imagination, she could almost feel her parents and grandparents sitting in the center of the auditorium smiling at her, encouraging her, telling her to go on.

Rosetta an arm's reach away from her, Ms. Jackson turned to the audience and said, "All right, everyone, the fifth grade class has a real treat for you." She faced Rosetta. "Ms. Blay," she said graciously, extending her hands towards Rosetta. Then, Ms. Jackson moved away from the microphone. She stepped back, to the stage's edge, just in front of the drapes.

Rosetta walked behind the tall microphone, filling the spot that Ms. Jackson had previously occupied. "Ladies and gentlemen," Rosetta began, her knees knocking, voice cracking.

"Ladies and gentlemen," kids near the front of the auditorium mimicked. They laughed. "We aren't ladies and gentlemen. We're kids."

Rosetta's supersonic ears picked up the mimicking. She hung her head for a second, but only for a second. "My fellow students," Rosetta pushed out her chest and grinned, her spunk back in full swing. She pointed toward her fifth grade classmates and cued them to circle around her.

From the tallest to the shortest, the fifth grade class circled Rosetta like she was a queen.

Grinning wildly, Rosetta began, "Do you know where you come from—"

All at once and out of nowhere, a loud "Ka-boom!" shook the auditorium.

The fifth graders froze, daring not to look down.

Rosetta was on the floor, her heart racing, her legs criss-crossed. Tears pooled in her eyes. She braced her chest. Her hands were shaking. She couldn't believe what was happening. She wondered if she had tripped, but no, she thought. She'd felt a hand against her back. If she didn't know any better, she would have sworn that someone had pushed her, just like Ellen had pushed her on the school bus.

Mrs. Greene sprang from her chair.

Mr. Perez, a science teacher, placed his hand on Mrs. Greene's forearm and encouraged her to return to her seat. "Let Ms. Jackson handle it," he told Mrs. Greene.

Ms. Jackson rushed across the stage to Rosetta's side. "Are you okay, Rosetta?" she asked.

Rosetta made her way to her knees. Then, she stood. She looked at Ms. Jackson, then she quickly turned away. Her knees were banging together the way that Bobby Jones had banged the drums for the seventh graders.

It had never mattered how embarrassed she felt, Rosetta Blay had always faced challenges head on. Her mother and father taught her that. They taught her to not allow fear to stop her from reaching her goals. They shared positive self-talk tricks with her, encouraging her to tell herself things like, "I can. I have what it takes. With the Creator there is nothing good that I cannot do and the Creator is always with me."

It worked . . . until now.

Everyone stared at Rosetta.

Rosetta glanced at Ms. Jackson. Then, Rosetta peered behind herself at Jennifer. Wrapping her hand around the microphone, Rosetta lowered the microphone so that it fit just beneath her mouth. It wasn't long before her back was straight and her head up. She looked like the true Rosetta Blay, strong, happy and assertive. "Ladies and gentlemen, my fellow students," she began again. "We have a rich history that is alive. That is why," she said with a snap of her head, "We are who we are, and we are wonderful."

No singing. No music. No dance. These fifth graders really are different, students in the audience thought.

A few students applauded. Every gaze was on Rosetta, the comeback kid.

"Every last one of us is a part of this," Rosetta said. And now--" Rosetta added, spreading her arms. She looked regal, like a queen preparing to introduce her subjects.

Ms. Jackson had moved back to the edge of the stage. She wore a hearty smile. She looked at Rosetta with so much pride that burgundy color went into her cheeks.

Jennifer looked from Ms. Jackson to the other fifth graders to Rosetta. Then, she looked out into the audience. She couldn't believe what she was witnessing. Her plan to destroy Rosetta's project was falling apart right in front of her eyes. And there wasn't anything that she could do. Her throat tightened.

She clenched her teeth and her jaw. She fought back tears. She didn't care how well Rosetta bounced back. She didn't care that Ellen hadn't been able to incite Rosetta toward trouble on the school bus. She didn't care that she hadn't been able to incite Rosetta to fight her in front of the entire class by pushing her to the floor. She, Jennifer Davis, wasn't going to be a part of this class project. She wasn't going to help her number one enemy, Rosetta Blay, not today, not ever.

"Ladies and gentlemen, students," Rosetta began. "Gregory Johnson," Rosetta bellowed, stepping toward the back of the stage.

Rosetta knew that she could call on Gregory first. He usually sat at the back of the fifth grade class. Gregory wasn't much of a talker, but he sure liked to laugh a lot. When he did talk, he was usually telling a joke. He was one of the kids in class who everyone liked.

Gregory was super cool.

Rosetta clapped while Gregory walked in front of her across the stage to the microphone.

Gregory held the stem of the microphone in his right hand. His left hand lay flat against his thigh. He swallowed hard several times while he stared out into the audience.

"My fellow students," Gregory began, his voice quavering, "I am here today to tell you about how my grandparents and parents," he said while he rocked from side to side on the backs of his heels, "and even my great-grandparents," he smiled, "impacted my life and helped me to be the person who I am today." He smiled. "But first, I want to read you a poem that I wrote about my family."

Students and teachers sitting in the auditorium leaned forward in their seats, eager to hear what Gregory would share.

Though the tree's roots are hidden

Powerful they are

Filling my days with hope, trust and strength

There's great-grandma Emma, Pop Pop Richard and Aunt Lena, a funny, short woman who always tells the truth

*There's Uncle Clyde, Uncle Malcolm and Grandma
Doris, her voice like an angel's, strong and
beautiful*

Parts of each of them are in me

*It's in my laugh, the jokes I love to tell and my love
of science and traveling to new, exciting places*

How glad I am that this tree will go on and on

It's why I want to do my best

As hard as it is for me to believe

*With each move that I make, I am adding to the
strength of my family tree*

Because years later

Like me

*Others will need the strength from the root to
thrive*

Gregory raised his voice and said, "My great-grandmother's name is Emma." His eyes lit up. The look on Gregory's face made everyone want to hear more.

"Great-grandma Emma was a grassroots leader during the Civil Rights Movement. "

Mrs. Greene snapped to attention. As a teenager, she'd participated in Civil Rights marches and restaurant sit-ins. She saw equality for all people as the only way to go. She hung onto every word that Gregory spoke.

Ms. Jackson leaned forward and focused on Gregory. She couldn't wait to hear what he was going to share next about his great-grandmother.

"Not only did Great-grandma Emma go to jail three times for working to integrate two restaurants in Mississippi when she was in high school, after she moved up North, she became a founding member of Shelby College in Cincinnati, Ohio."

Ewws and aahhhs sprinkled the auditorium, many of them coming from the mouths of teachers.

"Great-grandma Emma started Shelby College with a good friend named Leon." Gregory's smile widened. His eyes sparkled. "Leon went on to become my great-grandfather."

Laughter filled the auditorium.

Gregory spent another minute talking about his family. When he stepped back from the microphone, he was greeted with loud applause.

Rosetta clapped the loudest. Finally, the school project was getting off to a great start.

"Schoolmates," Rosetta said, walking to the microphone, "Remember that we each have two minutes to do our family presentations." She turned and looked down the stage. "Thank you, Gregory," she nodded, "for a wonderful start to our class project."

Another round of applause went up.

Lynette Sanchez went next. "My family is from San Juan, Puerto Rico," Lynette began. She wore a traditional red, blue and white bomba y plena set. A silk, red hibiscus flower was pinned to the right side of her shoulder length hair. "My paternal grandparents, Ian and Valeria Sanchez, still live in San Juan," she shared. "So do my maternal grandparents, Sebastian and Adriana Burgos," Lynette continued.

"San Juan was founded by Juan Ponce de Leon in 1521," Lynette told the school. "As a little girl, my mother loved visiting Luis Munoz Rivera Park. My mother, Clarita Sanchez, is active in the National Conference of Puerto Rican Women. My father, Luis Sanchez, is the owner of Sanchez Architecture which is located in downtown Cincinnati."

"My mother and my grandmothers cook the most delicious papas rellenas, pasteles and pollo guisado," Lynette smiled. "The meat is tender and taste so good," she added, her smile widening.

"I always love to visit my grandparents in San Juan. It's a beautiful city with shops, places to eat and it's near the ocean," Lynette told everyone. "We like to attend the La Campechada Festival in Ponce. It's in May," Lynette chuckled. Then, she laughed, spun in a full circle, sending the bottom of her wide skirt outward, and walked off the stage.

"Thank you, Lynette," Rosetta beamed. "Yours was a great presentation! And, now," Rosetta said, facing the audience. "Here's Anil Kumar."

"Hello, students and faculty," Anil began. He wore a silk, navy blue sherwani and a white dhoti. "My family is from New Delhi, India. I was two years old when we moved to the United States. My grandfather, Raj Kumar, is a farmer in New Delhi. He works hard farming rice, wheat and potatoes," Anil said. "My grandmother, Anita Basu, is really good with crafts like painted wood tables, wood face masks and rugs. She sells her goods at the Janpeth Market and the Khan Market. The markets are busy places with lots of cars, people and shops."

"New Delhi is huge. It's a lot bigger than New York City. More than twenty million people live in New Delhi. My family visits New Delhi once every two years," Anil said. "It's a really long flight. The flight is longer than seventeen hours," Anil laughed.

"Ewwws" sprinkled the auditorium.

"If we fly into Chicago or New York, it can take almost an entire day to get to India," Anil said. "Once in India, I've taken cart rides on Brahma bulls through markets. Those rides are similar to horse and buggy rides in the United States," Anil said.

"My mother's name is Sunita Singh. She is a marketing manager at Telepex in downtown Cincinnati. Telepex is a technology company. They make laptops, tablets, cell phones and software applications," Anil smiled.

"My father, Ashok Kumar, is a surgeon at Cincinnati Memorial Hospital. He also operates his own private medical practice. Both of my parents are busy people which is why I'm happy that my older brother, Manoj, is home. Manoj attends Josiah Henson High School. He's a junior this year."

"Everyone in my family is kind. Education is very important to my parents and grandparents. I have to do really well in school," Anil said. "Family is very important. Decisions, education and jobs that my parents and grandparents have made continue to help me and my brother, Manoj," Anil nodded, stepping away from the microphone. "Thank you for letting me tell you a little about my family history," Anil added just before he walked off stage.

One by one, Rosetta introduced the students in her class. Thanks to the presentations, students and teachers learned about Israel, Ghana, Africa, Scotland, Jamaica, California and Indiana. They also learned a lot about Ohio. Some of the students read poems or showed off colorful paintings. Other students showed family pictures and short, funny videos while they told stories about their family. Half an hour later, when she stepped to the microphone, Rosetta talked about her own family.

"My Grandma Fleming is one of my best friends," Rosetta began, her face lighting up. "No one is nicer or braver than she is." Rosetta pulled her hands behind her back, rocked from foot to foot and blushed. "She's a good cook too."

She glanced at Leroy then at Francine. They looked at her with as much curiosity as the other students did.

Rosetta continued. "When I asked my mother about Grandma Fleming, my mother told me that Grandma Fleming is courageous," Rosetta beamed. "Mommy said that Grandma Fleming has always been courageous, since my mother was a little girl. My mother told me that Grandma Fleming was active in the Civil Rights Movement too. She worked at NAACP offices throughout Cincinnati and in Kentucky and other Southern cities that she and Pop Pop Fleming traveled to in the 1960s."

"Grandma and Pop Pop Fleming didn't wait to see what others would do to make our communities better. No. No," Rosetta added with a shake of her head. "Pop Pop and Grandma Fleming rode the bus to Southern cities where they marched with Civil Rights leaders. When Pop Pop and Grandma Fleming came back to Cincinnati, they continued their work to make sure that everyone had access to equal rights, a good education and fairness in the courts and other places in America."

She took in a deep breath then let it go. "Nanny and Grandpa Blay are more sophisticated than my Grandma and Pop Pop Fleming."

Chuckles sprinkled the auditorium.

"They made sure that my father and his brothers and sisters were raised right. Nanny and Grandpa Blay had rules. They still do," Rosetta blurted. "They made sure that their kids kept those rules." She searched for words to speak. She didn't know her father's side of the family as well as she knew her mother's side of the family.

"The way that he was raised made my father responsible. That's what my father told me." She took in a deep breath. "My mother is the same way. They make a good couple which has made me and my sister smart and strong."

Rosetta looked at Leroy. "And my brother, Leroy, loads of fun. We get into trouble sometimes," she added while she grinned at Leroy. "But we do pretty good and our parents only stand for so much foolishness."

Laughter sprinkled throughout the auditorium.

Rosetta continued, "My family is from Virginia . . ." Moments later, Rosetta said, "So, as you can see, I wouldn't be who I am if it wasn't for my parents, my grandparents and other relatives." She paused. "Because of the time limits, none of us has long enough to talk about all of our relatives and how they influenced us. Yet, our lives show it. And when we all come together--" She spread her arms. "--we can see how our ancestors impact our school and our communities. And sometimes," she continued, "We have to try to understand each other better so that we can understand why we act and talk the way that we do." She glanced toward the left side of the stage at Ms. Jackson. "Because," she said while she peered at Jennifer, "the more we know about our own and other people's roots, the more we understand what makes us tick and what makes other people tick. That way, we can have less misunderstandings and maybe even come to like people who before we couldn't stand."

Ms. Jackson's spine stiffened. She glanced at Jennifer and hoped for the best.

"And now," Rosetta said. "Here is our last student to present." She paused. "Jennifer Davis."

Jennifer took her time getting to the microphone, walking in small steps, moving as slow as a snail. She didn't care if Rosetta was trying to be nice. To Jennifer, even when Rosetta tried to act like she had good manners, she was still rude. Jennifer knew that Rosetta didn't have to point her out the way that she did. All that talk about wanting to get to know someone better, and then talking about people who she used to not be able to stand. *"Well,"* Jennifer thought. *"I can't stand you either. I never could stand you, you dumb Rosetta Blay, and I can't stand you now."* She shook her head. *"I'm never going to stand you."*

"Thank you," Jennifer spoke politely into the microphone. She stepped in front of Rosetta. When she did, she jabbed Rosetta's chin with her elbow.

Next, Jennifer stepped to the right and blocked Rosetta, hiding Rosetta's frame, making it look as if Rosetta had disappeared.

Ms. Jackson saw Jennifer jab Rosetta. But she chalked it up to an accident. She knew that Jennifer was a well raised and respectable young lady, the kind of girl that she wished was her daughter.

Rosetta's brow furrowed. Her jaw was growing tight. She stared at Jennifer's back so hard that her eyes started to hurt.

Jennifer felt the heat from Rosetta's glare, but she never minded it. In fact, it made her feel good to know that she'd upset Rosetta. She leaned her head to the side. "Thank you, Ms. Rosetta Blay," she said real lady like.

From her seat in the audience, Mrs. Greene raised a brow. Something in Jennifer's voice didn't sound authentic to her.

"Teachers and fellow students," Jennifer said, "I'm not going to go over the time limit." She shot Rosetta a telling glance. "Even though there is so much to tell about my amazing family," she added. "But I do want you all to know that my family is from Ghana. That's in West Africa," Jennifer made clear. She said it as if she was the only person in the entire school who knew that Ghana was in West Africa.

"My ancestors were kings and queens in Africa. We never were enslaved," she said. "When my people came to America, we went straight North and set up our own businesses. We owned land." She smiled. "Two of my uncles own farms right to this day. My grandmother Howard, my father's mother, was a school teacher at a private college, one of the first colleges for African Americans," she said.

"My grandfather Howard owned his own construction company. He built a lot of houses right here in Cincinnati," she said. "My grandfather and grandmother Richardson, my mother's parents, own an Art gallery close to the University of Cincinnati. Years ago, their gallery was used to hold Civil Rights meetings. My grandparents Richardson ate dinner with great Civil Rights leaders back in the 1960s."

"My mother remembers those dinners," Jennifer smiled. "She tells me how lively and interesting the conversations around the dinner table were back then. My family is a very close family," Jennifer continued. "We support each other. We strive to be independent land owners and business starters." She longed to glance at Ms. Jackson to see if her presentation met with her approval. She wanted to see in Ms. Jackson's eyes that her presentation was the best of all the student presentations. But, even more, she didn't want to let on that she cared what Ms. Jackson or anyone thought of her. So, she didn't turn and look.

"You see, my family . . ." Jennifer continued.

Five minutes later, Rosetta glanced at her watch. She huffed and rolled her eyes.

"We are a strong people who have made a lot of contributions to this community, to this great nation, to Africa. . ."

Students yawned and stretched in their seats. A few teachers squirmed in the audience.

"I can only imagine what I would be like, what my beautiful sister, Gloria, and my two strong brothers, Mark and Kevin, would be like if it wasn't for our parents, grandparents and our other amazing ancestors. . ." Jennifer droned on.

Rosetta tapped her foot against the floor. Then, she rolled her eyes. "Come on," she mouthed.

Ms. Jackson shot Rosetta a glance. She knew that Jennifer had gone far beyond the time limit, but she didn't interrupt Jennifer. She didn't want to embarrass her. After all, she hadn't embarrassed or interrupted any of the other students. She didn't even say anything when Billie Anderson belched in the middle of his presentation. She didn't say anything when Lynette Sanchez started giggling near the end of her presentation. She didn't say anything when Belinda Franklin waved to her friend Joann in the sixth grade while she gave her presentation.

Ten minutes later, Jennifer was still talking. "Even today, there's a village in Ghana named after my great-great-great . . ."

Chapter Ten

Chatter filled the Blay kitchen. Cheese broccoli, sliced tomatoes, steamed kale, baked grouper and macaroni and cheese were placed in bowls on the table. Hot steam and the sweetest smells billowed off the food.

The kitchen was alive with laughter and lighthearted conversation. Then, Rosetta's mother, Lynda, hushed everyone and asked the big question. "Rosetta, how was the school project?"

Francine didn't give Rosetta time to answer. "Ro did great," she exclaimed.

Rosetta's father looked at Francine with raised brows. Then, he looked at Rosetta. He could hardly believe what he was hearing. "I should record this," he teased. "Francine paying Rosetta a compliment." He grinned. Then, he started to laugh.

Lynda laughed with him. "Now, that is something," she said.

Francine wrapped her arm around Rosetta's shoulder, something that she only did when Rosetta got picked on in school by an older kid and she felt sorry for her. "I love Ro."

"Rosetta was the bo-diggity," Leroy said. "She held it down."

"She talked about our family like we were down to earth, but also like we were great people. I felt so proud while Ro was up on stage talking," Francine said. "I missed part of her speech when I got up to use the bathroom, but I liked what I heard."

"Rosetta told the truth in a real cool way," Leroy added. He started to clap. "You did excellently, Ro," he told her.

Lynda ate a forkful of the green leafy kale. "How did the rest of the class do? Were you a good organizer and leader, Rosetta?" She washed the kale down with a swig of lemonade.

"I did all right," Rosetta said. She stared into her plate. The broken tomato slices reminded her of her arch nemesis. "Jennifer—"

Robert grinned. He tapped his wife's forearm with the point of his elbow. "Mrs. Greene called about Jennifer," he told Rosetta.

"She sure did," Lynda said. "She told us how professional and courteous you were, even after Jennifer poked you and didn't apologize."

"You know," Robert said. "Like your mother and I tell you, sometimes when you keep doing the right thing, the right thing happens."

Lynda raised a finger. "That's true. You might have to wait and put in some work. But if you keep doing what's right and thinking and living in love, good comes."

"Yeah," Rosetta said. "But I can hardly believe that Mrs. Greene called. She never thinks I'm the one who didn't start the trouble."

"Well, this time she saw what happened while she was sitting in the audience," Robert said. "She also mentioned something about you being pushed to the floor. I think that's what really prompted her to call. She probably thought that you'd run home and tell us what happened and that we'd call the school first thing tomorrow morning." He glanced at his wife and laughed. "Probably figured that she'd beat us to the punch."

"What about Ms. Jackson?" Rosetta wanted to know. She grinned with hope. "Did she call?"

"Not yet," Lynda answered. "But even if Ms. Jackson doesn't call, Mrs. Greene knows what was going on, and besides that," Lynda added, "Did you learn anything wonderful and new about Jennifer while she gave her presentation?"

"I learned that she likes to talk about herself and her family," Leroy interrupted.

"She sure does," Francine chimed. "Jennifer likes to brag on herself."

"Ro, maybe you should try to make friends with her," Lynda suggested.

Rosetta's eyes swelled. "Are you kidding?" Her lemonade almost spilled out of her mouth, she was so shocked at her mother's suggestion.

"No. I'm serious," Lynda said. "Sounds to me like Ms. Jennifer doesn't feel sure about herself. She might be helped if you make friends with her and let her know that she's good and wonderful all by herself. That way you might notice that she stops bragging and trying to make herself appear to be heads above other people."

"Yes," Robert added. "I've found that when people set themselves apart it's usually because they don't feel like they measure up, like they belong. Now, I know," he said. "That can cause a person to seem arrogant. But what the person usually is really feeling is small and left out."

"Right," Lynda nodded.

Rosetta sat back against her chair. Not once did she think about Jennifer's report card or compare herself against Jennifer's grades.

Pondering her family's comments, Rosetta let out a deep breath. "I don't know," she said. "For now, I just want to enjoy the success of the fifth grade school talent show project, and," she was quick to add, "how well Leroy and Francine and all of the students did in all of the talent show presentations today."

"All right," Robert and Lynda cheered.

Each member of the family raised their glasses and clinked them together at the center of the table. "Cheers," they all sang.

Beneath the kitchen table the family dog, Joe, barked and wagged his tail.

Made in the USA
Coppell, TX
06 January 2022

70679042R00066